Toshiden

Exploring Japanese Urban Legends
Vol. 2

Tara A. Devlin

Toshiden: Exploring Japanese Urban Legends Vol. 2
First Edition: May 2019

taraadevlin.com

DEDICATION

To everyone who wanted another volume of this craziness. Thank you.

CONTENTS

Introduction

1 Supernatural 1

2 Society 89

3 Medical 129

4 Entertainment 163

5 Jokes 217

6 Crime 235

INTRODUCTION

When I released *Toshiden: Exploring Japanese Urban Legends Vol. 1* in 2018, I wasn't sure how the book would be received. I've loved urban legends since I was a child, but how would other people feel about a book that didn't just look at the stories of Japanese legends, but their histories, their origins, and their variations? Thankfully, people took to it very well! I received numerous requests and comments asking if and when a second volume would be coming out.

Here it is!

If you've read the first volume of *Toshiden*, you'll know what to expect here. The book is split into sections featuring urban legends not just of the supernatural variety, but also from society at large, medical oddities, dark secrets from the entertainment industry, punny jokes, and horrific crimes all straight out of Japan. All research comes straight from Japanese sources and looks at the development of these legends, how they came to be in the first place, whether they are true or not, and interesting variations you can find in different areas of Japan.

So, without further ado, get ready to feel your skin crawl. Get ready to laugh. Get ready to think. Get ready to cringe. This volume has it all! Welcome to *Toshiden: Exploring Japanese Legends Vol. 2*!

SUPERNATURAL

Sukima-onna

A young man lived all alone. One day, he felt someone looking at him from within his room. He looked around but, of course, nobody was there. There was no reason for anyone else to be there but him. And yet, the feeling that someone was looking at him continued.

Worried, the young man searched his room, but he found nothing. It was possible that someone was peeping at him from outside, but his curtains were closed, so there was no way to see in. Maybe someone had installed a surveillance camera, or a listening device… He got even more worried, and carefully searched through every inch of his room. Then, he found the source of the gaze.

In the thin gap between the dresser and the wall, a woman was staring right at him…

ABOUT

There's a good chance you've heard of Sukima-onna, or the Gap Woman, before. She's a favourite of 2chan, and her popularity has spread to Western shores as well. At her most basic, Sukima-onna is a woman that peers out from the gaps in one's room. Any gaps. It can be from between the dresser and wall, as in the above story, or it can be from underneath the bed, behind the curtain, in the drawers… absolutely anywhere. There's no gap too small for her, and the only way to avoid her gaze is to make sure that every single little gap is covered. That means even the cracks in the floor, wall, or doors. Everything. You'll need a lot of tape, if the idea of her gazing at you from every nook and cranny doesn't drive you insane first.

Gaps were once thought to connect this world to the next, but where did she originally come from?

HISTORY

In modern times, Sukima-onna gained popularity when comedian Sakura Kinzo told her story to the masses on the daytime television show *Waratte Iitomo*. His version, called the "One Millimetre Ghost" or "One Millimetre Woman," went as follows:

> A certain man didn't show up to work one day. Worried, his colleague called him, but was unable to get in contact with him. A week passed without word from the man, and so his colleagues went to his apartment to find out what was going on.
>
> When they got there, the man was inside. When they asked what was going on, the man informed his colleagues that he hadn't taken a single step outside all week.
>
> "It's not healthy to stay inside for so long," one of his colleagues told him.
>
> "She gets lonely, so I can't go out," the man replied.
>
> Confused, his colleagues asked him, "What are you talking about? There's no woman here."
>
> Then, one of the workers pointed behind the dresser in the room. "She's in there…"

> When they looked, they found a woman in a red dress standing in the gap between the dresser and the wall. She was staring right at them.
>
> The colleagues ran, and nobody ever found out what happened to the man after that.

Yet Sukima-onna's origins begin even earlier than this. Her story can be traced all the way back to *Mimibukuro*, written by Negishi Yasumori, a samurai who worked in a senior administrative position during the latter years of the Edo Period. Negishi collected anecdotes and strange stories from various people, including his colleagues and the elderly, over a period of 30 years. He then collected these stories into 10 different volumes of 100 stories each which he called *Mimibukuro*. One of the stories he collected is nearly word-for-word the story of Sukima-onna that we know today:

> A young man lived alone, and he could sense somebody looking upon him in his room. Of course, there was nobody in the room but him. He thought he was probably just imagining things, so he soon forgot about it.
>
> However, starting from that day, the boy felt like someone was watching him; day in, day out. He lived on the second floor, so it was difficult to think that someone might be looking in from the outside. He started to think someone was hiding inside the room, so he began his search, but of course, it was all for nothing. He thought he was going insane.
>
> One day, when he felt himself succumbing to

> such thoughts again, he finally found the source of the gaze. A woman was standing in the few millimetres between his dresser and the wall, and she was staring right at him.

Sukima-onna has changed little over the years, a rare yokai that finds herself able to comfortably fit into any time period without major revisions.

VARIATIONS

She's not without variations, however. Some tales also tell of Sukima-otoko, the Gap Man. Depending on the story, Sukima-otoko and Sukima-onna can be interchangeable, but one variation goes as follows:

> The ordinary places people live are full of innumerable gaps. In those gaps resides Sukima-otoko, and it's said that if you happen to meet his gaze, he will drag you off to a different dimension. You will never be able to return home again.
>
> In other cases, someone will suddenly approach you from behind and say, "Let's play hide and seek." You must hide, but when Sukima-otoko finds you, he will drag you off to another world.

In stories exclusive to Sukima-otoko, it's said the middle of his forehead, the area between his brows, has been smashed open. No reason has ever been given as to why.

In other versions, Sukima-onna likes to hide in

different areas of the house:

> One hot summer's day, a young man was watching TV at home alone. It was just past one in the morning and he suddenly felt thirsty, so he made his way into the dark kitchen. Light from the living room filtered in, so he was able to see well enough without turning the lights on.
>
> He grabbed a can of beer from the fridge, closed the door… and then he saw it.
>
> A woman, standing in the 10 cm gap between the fridge and the wall.
>
> He screamed, and the woman disappeared. After that, the young man avoided using the kitchen at night. Just who was that woman?

She also doesn't necessarily have to be super thin:

> A man discovered a rather cheap apartment in the heart of Tokyo. Compared to nearby units, this one was three times cheaper, and when the man asked the real estate to show him around inside, he found no problems with it.
>
> "How lucky! What a bargain!"
>
> "We don't often get places like this," the real estate said. "The landlord asked us to rent it at this price, but there are people who would pay much more for it."
>
> The man decided to move in.
>
> The first day he moved in he found it extremely comfortable. There was a convenience store just outside, and he was just a four-minute

walk from the closest station. After he was done unpacking and putting away his stuff, he was overcome with exhaustion. He lay down on the sofa and fell asleep.

When he woke up, it was past 3 a.m.

"Crap. I'll catch a cold sleeping here," he said. He lay his futon out, but something felt off. He was alone in the room, but he could sense someone else in there with him. Or to put it more correctly, he could feel someone looking at him.

No. It was just his imagination. He brushed it off and went back to sleep. But the next day, and the day after that, he continued to feel someone's gaze upon him.

Someone was watching him.

He checked every nook and cranny of the room, but he couldn't find anyone else in there. Then one day, after returning home from work, he found a book from the shelf on the sofa. It was a book he'd bought 10 years earlier; he had no reason to be reading it now.

Anxiety rose within him.

He set up four cameras in the room, so he could see every single corner of it. The cameras ran all day long. He left for work.

When he got home, he checked the video feed. Nobody was there. He lived alone, so of course no-one else was there, but he carefully checked over all the footage.

Maybe it really was his imagination? Was he just tired? Come to think of it, his entire living environment had changed, so maybe his exhaustion had been building up without him noticing.

He watched the footage absentmindedly, but then he noticed something unbelievable change on the screen before him. The closet door slowly began to open. It was so slow that it appeared to be happening in slow motion. He didn't understand it. Then, slowly, an unknown woman with blank eyes stepped out and looked around the room.

That very closet was right behind him. He didn't have the strength to turn around and look at it. He broke out into a cold sweat. His entire body stiffened. A silence fell over the room. He prepared himself to run.

Then. From behind…

"You noticed me, huh?"

He heard an unknown woman's voice.

This particular story might bring up images of the real news story that broke in 2008 of a 58-year-old woman who was found living in a man's closet in Fukuoka for close to a year. The man installed security cameras after he noticed food going missing, and she was discovered emerging from the closet after he left to eat and use his shower. She slipped into the house when the man left the door unlocked one day, and police believed that she had squatted in other people's houses as well. Police found her still huddled in the top of the closet when they came to search the house and arrested her for trespassing.

METHOD OF ATTACK AND ESCAPE

As we can see from the above Sukima-onna stories, she has various methods of attack. Sometimes it's left up to the listener's imagination what she does with her victims, but often she keeps them contained to their house, unable to leave her behind, or she takes them off to another dimension entirely. Colleagues or friends who visit the victim will find them fading away, unable to leave to buy food, and not having moved or exercised since the last time anyone saw them. Only a husk of a human remains, and unfortunately, if you happen to see Sukima-onna on your visit as well, she might transfer herself to you like a virus, and you'll find your apartment haunted next.

So, how can you deal with her?

As is often the case with yokai in urban legends, you can't. Not really. You can cover all the gaps in your house with packing tape, but it's not a very practical way to live, nor is it guaranteed that you'll seal every single crack. She can appear in the tiniest areas that the human eye might easily miss, and it ultimately amounts to putting a plaster on a knife wound. You might succeed in covering it, but it's still festering away under the surface, threatening to break free and bleed all over the floor at any moment.

Some have suggested that you can lure Sukima-onna to another house, although no successful method has ever been given. Some versions of the tale mention that seeing her is enough for her to start haunting you, but if you think inviting your friends around to get her off your case will help, beware; she generally won't move on until the person she's haunting is already dead. Sorry.

TRUTH BEHIND HER POPULARITY

When people discover the victims of Sukima-onna, a few things stand out: they are weak, exhausted, they haven't eaten or moved in days, and find themselves unable to leave their house. While women have been known to fall victim to her, the majority are young men. Do these symptoms sound familiar? One suggestion for Sukima-onna's rise in popularity in modern times is that she reflects a common sickness that often goes undiagnosed in Japan today: chronic fatigue syndrome (CFS).

It's said that three out of every thousand people in Japan potentially have CFS, with 3% of those being women. Most, however, are mis- or undiagnosed, with many cases being treated as a psychosomatic illness or depression instead. Those suffering from CFS may appear lazy, unmotivated, or as skipping out on work/social events for no real reason. Sukima-onna may be symbolic of the times, an attempt at explaining why many young men appear so exhausted and unwilling to leave the house.

MEDIA

A film titled *Sukima-onna* was released in 2014. In it, a young office worker named Koharu hears that something strange has happened to her estranged younger sister, Kyoko. She visits her apartment and finds all the gaps covered in packing tape, and her sister weak with exhaustion. Kyoko explains that she went to a certain house for a test of courage—a house that was supposed to be haunted by the evil spirit known as "Sukima-onna"—and now she's fallen under her curse. Koharu visits the house to learn more in an attempt to help her sister and discovers someone new has moved in, and she's being locked inside by Sukima-onna as well…

A light novel by Maruyama Hideto called *Sukima-onna (Wide Width)* was released in 2009. In the story, a Sukima-onna by the name of Harimi (using the kanji for "beautiful needle") gets caught between the dresser and wall of a young man named Takumi. Harimi has a fondness for human food, and her overeating has led to her becoming "wide width," or the size of a normal human being. The story examines the relationship between the two as they learn to co-exist in the same room and, in contrast to the horror the original legend might suggest, also comes with a happy ending.

Sukima-onna's popularity continues to grow, and for a yokai that has been around since the Edo Period, she just seems to be hitting her stride. After all, the modern world is full of tiny gaps. You never know where she might be…

Human-faced Dog

A young man was working late at night at a restaurant. It was about time to close, so he carried the kitchen garbage out the back door to the trash as he always did. The back door faced a narrow alley, and being that it was late, there was no pedestrian traffic.

"There's a dog going through the rubbish…"

When he looked over, a single dog had its head thrust in the restaurant's trash, rummaging through it. Thinking it a nuisance that would run away if he approached it, the man dragged his large bag of rubbish over.

Most wild dogs would run away at the sight of a human, but this one continued to give its undivided attention towards the trash. Not wanting the dog to scatter the restaurant's garbage any further, the young man yelled at the dog.

"Hey! Quit making a mess!"

The dog slowly turned to look at him. But it wasn't a dog. Its body was that of a dog, but its face was human…

ABOUT

The legend of the human-faced dog, or *jinmen inu* in Japanese, started to spread across Japan in the late 1980s, particularly amongst elementary school students. It became so popular that it caused a swath of "human-faced" legends to emerge, with tales of human-faced fish and human-faced spiders, amongst others. If you could think of it, there was probably a tale of a human-faced version somewhere. But where did it come from, and why was the human-faced dog so popular?

HISTORY

Legends of where the human-faced dog came from are almost as varied and famous as the original tale itself. In 1973, Tsunoda Jiro published a manga called *Ushiro no Hyakutaro*. One of the characters was a ghostly dog named "Zero," who communicated telepathically with the protagonist and possessed a human face. A few years later, in 1978, the movie *Invasion of the Body Snatchers* was released, which also featured a dog with a human face. Dogs with human faces were clearly not a new idea, but these may have planted the first seeds in the public imagination of the legend that was yet to come.

One popular theory for how the human-faced dog came to be can be found in the inaugural issue of *Quick Japan* magazine. *Quick Japan* published a report stating that journalist Ishimaru Gensho, then a writer for the magazine *Popteen*, colluded with *Popteen*'s editorial department over a reader-submitted story. That story was about a human-faced dog. He took the story—without publishing it—and expanded on it to create his own work. It was *this* story that then created the human-faced dog boom of the early 1990s.

Japanese actor Matoba Koji later appeared on the nighttime television show *Downtown DX*, and there he claimed that he and his friends often joked about stray dogs with human faces. This made human-faced dog stories even more popular, helping the legend spread further.

On the radio program *Bakusho Mondai Cowboy*, comedian Tanaka Yuji told a story from one of his friends that claimed to be the origin of the urban legend. According to him, an urban legend club at a certain university in Tokyo wanted to research how legends spread amongst young children. They created fake posters and went around asking children about the human-faced dog, deliberately spreading misinformation. While wearing white lab coats, they asked elementary school students, "A dog with a human face has escaped from the research centre, have you seen it?" These same university students supposedly added an ending to the story that featured the dog saying "leave me alone" in response to people approaching it.

Furthermore, in 1988, the TBS radio program *Super Gang: Teens Dial* featured a special on the human-faced dog. This particular show had a large influence on spreading the legend around the country, and over 150 people called in that very same night to report they had seen a human-faced dog in the flesh. So many people called in that many were left on hold, unable to get through.

Whether any of these stories, or a mix of these stories, are the true origin, nobody has yet come to an agreement on. Tales of creatures possessing a human face, such as the kudan (a human-faced cow), or the nue (a mixture of various creatures, much like a chimera, and sometimes said to possess human features) have been around for hundreds of years. In fact, in the book *Gaidan Bunbun Shuyo*, written by author Ishizuka Hokaishi in 1810, he tells the tale of a dog in the town of Tadocho, Edo, who gave birth to a puppy with a human face. A showman catches wind of the strange birth and buys the puppy to put in his show, selling out crowds with its incredible popularity. There was a real-life superstition at the time that intercourse with a female dog would cure syphilis, which led to rumours and tales of puppies being born with human faces.

According to fellow Edo writer Kato Ebian, on April 29, 1819, a puppy was born in the Nihonbashi area with a human face that became the talk of the town. Folks who told him the tale said the dog had a face like that of a monkey. Some tile block prints made during the era also portrayed these human-faced dogs as having human front legs to go with their faces.

VARIATIONS

There are two main stories told about the human-faced dog. The first and main story is the one mentioned earlier. Some versions of this tale go a little further, with the dog turning to look at the man with an exhausted look on his face and saying "Leave me alone," like the version supposedly spread by university students. He's also been known to mutter "I'm free to do what I want," "Shut up," or "Oh, it's just a human."

Other versions have the dog able to jump over six metres into the air on the spot, and in some, the dog is actually an escaped experiment from a research facility.

The other main version of the story claims that if you overtake a human-faced dog while driving on the highway, you will crash and potentially die. Here, the dog is able to reach speeds of 100 kilometres per hour and will chase down cars, generally causing them to crash. Some origin stories for the dog claim he actually died in a car accident, and the human-faced dog is his spirit.

According to yokai researcher Yamaguchi Bintaro, a lesser known version states that a middle-aged businessman committed suicide after he lost his job in a company downsizing, and through his malice, was possessed by a dog spirit, causing him to become a human-faced dog. It's also said that if a human-faced dog bites you, you will become one yourself, much like a strange human-canine vampire with a taste for trash.

Depending on who you want to believe, the human-faced dog is either an angry spirit (human or canine, sometimes both), a yokai, or a biological experiment gone wrong. Some legends even claim the dog was created by mutation thanks to environmental pollution!

CHARACTERISTICS

Popteen ran a "Final Human-Faced Dog Report" in their April 1989 issue, where they gathered data from people all around the country who claimed to have seen the animal. They concluded the following:

- Only people with a strong *reikan*, or ability to see ghosts, were able to see the human-faced dog. If two people were together, there was no guarantee that both people would see it.
- There isn't just one human-faced dog. Several were seen all over the country by numerous people.
- The human-faced dogs knew they were being talked about. One second grade high school student from Kawagoe City in Saitama Prefecture claimed that one approached her to talk. She worked up the courage to ask it what it really was, and claimed the dog answered, "I can't say right now, but now that everyone is talking about us, daily life has become more difficult."
- Human-faced dogs never attacked people. Not a single person who came across them mentioned they had been directly attacked by the dogs.

THE HIDDEN TRUTH

One theory has been suggested for the human-faced dog's popularity in modern times. It's not just the shocking image of a human face on a dog's body, nor the continuation of a creature supposedly seen since the times of Edo. Rather, this depiction of a human confined to the body of a dog represents the feeling of young people's restricted freedoms. It's almost always young people who claim to see the dog, and while the dog itself may not really exist, the feelings behind what it represents do.

The dog is famous for saying “Leave me alone,” “Shut up,” and “I can do what I want.” Sounds like something a teenager might say, right? Thus, those who claim to have seen the human-faced dog, of course, have not seen it, but are instead venting their frustrations at society and the rules imposed upon them by putting themselves in the role of the dog with a human face.

Even Though You Can See Me

Three university students were walking down a busy street. One of them looked up and saw a man in military uniform leaning against a building. He appeared to be in pain, but was doing his best to endure it… At least, that was what she thought. Perhaps a television program was filming nearby and he was just an extra. That had to be it.

But strangely, neither her two friends walking beside her, nor anybody else on the street seemed to notice him. The girl grew scared and avoided looking at him as they walked by. Then, just as she passed him, she heard the man mutter.

"Even though you can see me…"

ABOUT

It's thought that this story was first told on television by a popular idol, although nobody seems to remember who or even when. Japanese celebrities spend a lot of time sharing funny and scary stories on television, so it's not uncommon to attribute stories to them without remembering who exactly it was, or even when someone heard it.

These days there are numerous versions of the same tale that all end with the ghostly figure saying to the girl passing by, "Even though you can see me…" The Japanese used, *mieteru kuse ni*, is rather accusatory in its tone. The ghost knows the girl can see him or her and is chiding her for pretending otherwise. It's a gentle reminder that for those who have the ability to see ghosts, it can be rather inconvenient sometimes, and once you notice something unnatural, there's no point in pretending otherwise. It knows, too.

VARIATIONS

Perhaps the most common variation of this legend involves the girl waiting at a set of traffic lights instead of walking past a soldier leaning on a building. It goes as follows:

> One night, a woman was waiting by some traffic lights on a busy street. The woman possessed a strong *reikan*, allowing her to see ghosts, and suddenly she felt a chill run down her spine. She noticed a woman standing on the other side of the street, waiting just like her. She was surrounded by people and there was nothing particularly strange about her, but something about the woman caught her eye.
>
> The lights turned green and people started crossing the road. The woman cast her eyes down to avoid looking at this other woman as she passed. Yet, when she approached the middle of the street and walked by, she heard her laugh.
>
> "Even though you can see me…"

Some versions combine these two, and the girl passes a soldier at the traffic lights instead. Further stories add another element of fear by having the ghost show up at the girl's home right as she's on the verge of forgetting anything ever happened.

That ending goes as follows:

> One year passed, and the woman was on the verge of forgetting about the man in military clothes she saw that day. Her doorbell rang, so the woman got up to answer it and saw the soldier standing on her doorstep with a gun. He fired twice, and the woman died.
>
> To all who hear this story, the man in the military clothes will show up on your doorstep within three days as well…

With this version, we see the common "to all who hear this story, they will meet the same fate" added in an attempt to have the tale passed around like a chain letter. It seems to have worked, because people are still talking about it even now.

Ski Resort

A man went on a trip to a ski resort. It was a weekday so there were few people around. Thinking it was a great chance to ski his heart out, he hit the slopes. He was enjoying himself immensely, but then he heard something coming from the forest next to the course.

The man approached it, wondering what it could be.

"Help me!"

This time he clearly heard a voice. He entered the forest and found the top half of a woman's body sticking out of the snow. She must have fallen into a hole.

"I'll get you out!" the man screamed. He grabbed her hands and pulled with all his might.

"What the…?"

The woman was lighter than he expected and he faced little resistance as he pulled her up. However, there was a reason she was so light. Where her lower body should have been, there was nothing. What the man thought was a hole was nothing more than a pile of snow.

The upper body of the woman he was holding grinned at him.

ABOUT

This story likely brings to mind Kashima Reiko, or Teketeke, other famous legends of women who are missing their lower halves. While this particular legend isn't as famous as those, it was likely inspired by them and makes for a neat little horror story all by itself.

The first evidence of this story online comes from a post on 2chan on August 3, 2007, in a thread of people sharing famous scary stories. It's unclear where this one originated from, or if it was created solely to share in the thread, but the original poster shared several scary stories that featured legs or a lack thereof. The story was then copied and shared around the internet until it became a legend in its own right. Although, considering the woman in this tale doesn't have a name, she's unlikely to ever reach the lofty heights of her predecessors Kashima-san and Teketeke, and the story remains known only as "Ski Resort."

Oshima

Tojinbo is known Japan-wide as a suicide spot, but nearby you'll find an island called Oshima. It's said that the bodies of those who jump from the Tojinbo cliffs wash up on Oshima. It's also said that if you walk counter-clockwise around the island, you'll open the gate to the underworld and get sucked in. This is the one rule the locals make sure to always adhere to.

ABOUT

Oshima is a real location you can find just off the coast of Mikuni in Fukui Prefecture. Like the legend states, the island is located just a short distance away from the Tojinbo cliffs, a famous suicide spot. It's connected to the mainland by a 100 metre long vermilion-lacquered bridge. There's not a lot on the island; some Shinto shrines, a spring, a lighthouse, and some great views. There's also a sign at the top of the stone steps once you enter the island that says "← Counter-clockwise Rotation". This route will take you around the island and back to the start again, and this particular rule to go left instead of right at the fork has been followed by the locals since long ago. Those who ignore this rule and turn right will face misfortune, calamity, and possibly even death.

Many of the people who jump from the Tojinbo cliffs are lost in the jagged rocks below, but the occasional body is swept away on the tide and washes up on Oshima a short distance away. For this reason, the locals have long believed Oshima to be haunted, and it's a popular spot for teenagers to test their courage.

This legend once featured on the television program *Unbelievable*, and starting the very next morning the island found itself flooded with tourists who wanted to see whether the rumours were true or not. Word of mouth spread that people were injured or fell ill after walking clockwise around the island, and its reputation grew. Walking clockwise leads one on a dangerous path to the other side, and that path can cause people to want to leap to their deaths from the jagged cliffs as well.

GOING RIGHT

But why is it forbidden to walk right? Why can't someone walk counter-clockwise around the island? There's a path that leads to the right, after all. What's the difference? According to one spirit medium, there are barriers around the island that people can't see if walking right, and these will obstruct their path. These invisible barriers are said to be the *jibakurei*, or ghosts tied to the island, who are trying to protect tourists from harm. But being told not to do something makes some people want to do it even more, and many tales—true or not—are told of people who travelled to the island with family or friends, went counter-clockwise around the island, and then soon after leaving were involved in horrific accidents. Even today these stories are still spread on the internet, and you don't have to look hard to find them.

One tale tells of an anonymous poster's older brother's friend who visited Oshima with two friends. They walked around the island not once but twice counter-clockwise. The next day, one of those friends crashed his scooter and ended up in hospital for a month with serious injuries. The other friend was rushed to hospital a few days later with urinary stones, and then the friend was involved in a car accident while at work.

But is this rule really that sinister, or just an old wives' tale to get people to stay in line? After all, if everyone is going in one direction and a few people decide to go the other way, they're bound to meet up and get in each other's way; which, on a place with as many sheer cliffs as Oshima, can be perilous.

FURTHER CURSES

There's another legend that states if you remove a stone from Oshima and take it home with you, you'll be cursed. Oshima is designated as a quasi-national park, and is therefore protected. It might seem obvious, but sometimes it takes a scary story to stop people from doing something they shouldn't. Some stories also claim that if you don't complete a full lap of the island after passing under the shrine gate, you'll be cursed. The entire island itself is home to Oominato Shrine, and is worshipped as a holy site by locals. If you're going to visit, it's probably best not to upset the various *kami* and ghosts that reside there. Be respectful, follow the path, don't take anything, and don't get cursed.

The Granny Who Sells Legs

One day after school, a young boy was approached by an old lady on his way home.

"Do you need legs? Do you need legs?"

The boy tried to ignore her and walk past, but she was unexpectedly persistent.

"Do you need legs? Do you need legs?" she asked him over and over.

"I don't need any legs!" the boy screamed in refusal.

"Ahhhhh!"

A scream rang throughout the street in the dim evening light. Hearing it, several people came running, but what they saw took their breath away. A young boy was crouching on the street, his legs plucked clean off.

ABOUT

The granny who sells legs is a fairly typical yokai, and may bring to mind images of Kashima-san, who also asks people if they need legs. In both cases, if the answer is "no," you'll find your legs cut off. You *did* say you didn't need legs, after all.

This strange old lady approaches people, particularly children, on the street as it's getting dark and asks, "Do you need legs?" as though she has some to sell. Of course, nobody wants to buy legs from a crazy old lady on the street, so when you answer "no," she takes that the literal way and plucks your legs off. If, however, you decide to answer "yes," then she will forcibly attach a third leg to your body. It's probably best not to imagine how or where. As is common with yokai, neither answer ends well.

There is only one way to escape the granny who sells legs. When she asks, "Do you need legs?" the correct answer is "No, I don't, but why don't you visit OO-san." By giving her somebody else's name and recommending she visit them, you'll be able to escape. Of course, the person you tell her to visit shouldn't be someone you like, because the same fate will befall them as well.

VARIATIONS

This legend became popular during the 1990s, although these days it's almost faded into obscurity. There is a similar legend called "The Granny Who Gives Legs" that is essentially the same story, but with the main difference being that this granny targets children who actually want legs. Some versions also have her appearing in the fourth floor toilets of various schools, dragging a wagon behind her (presumably full of the legs she's stolen from children).

In some stories she also wears a large cape on her back, and underneath it she hides the legs she's taken. This version likely came about because of the common sight of old women bent over, especially in the countryside. These women tend to suffer from osteoporosis after years of poor nutrition during and after the war, and after years of hard work in the fields. It's not much of a stretch to see how a child might see such a woman in the dim evening light and wonder what exactly is hidden under her coat.

Some versions of the legend even give the granny who sells legs a partner; the grandpa who sells arms. You probably don't have to guess how that one came around.

It's unknown how the legend of this particular yokai (or *yurei*, depending on who you talk to) came about, but it's likely she started as a joke legend because the idea of someone literally taking your legs when you say you don't need any is both terrifying and funny.

Kudan

Kudan is a yokai with the face of a human and the body of a cow. Soon after it's born it speaks with human speech, prophecising a great calamity to come, and then passes away. The kudan's prophecy always comes true, and is never wrong. They frequently appeared in the Edo Period, predicting famines, earthquakes, and volcanic eruptions. Before the Second World War, a kudan predicted its outbreak, and the last kudan born prophecised Japan's defeat.

ABOUT

The reason this yokai is called "kudan" is because of the Chinese character that makes up its name. Using the radical for person beside the character for cow, this character is read *kudan* in Japan, and so the cow with a human face was given the same name.

Kudan first appeared in the early half of the 19th century in Japan. While they are generally cows with a human face, after the Second World War, various stories of kudan with human bodies and cow faces started to appear as well. After they are born, they tell a prophecy of great misfortune to come, and then die a few days later. In some versions, they die immediately after.

Kudan exploded with popularity during the Meiji Period, and several supposedly real stuffed kudan appeared in exhibitions around the country. Lafcadio Hearn even wrote of it in his book

Glimpses of Unfamiliar Japan:

> What is a Kudan?
>
> It is possible you have never heard of the Kudan? The Kudan has the face of a man, and the body of a bull. Sometimes it is born of a cow, and that is a Sign-of-things-going-to-happen. And the Kudan always tells the truth. Therefore in Japanese letters and documents it is customary to use the phrase, Kudannno-gotoshi—"like the Kudan"—or "on the truth of the Kudan."
>
> But why was the God of Mionoseki angry about the Kudan?
>
> People said it was a stuffed Kudan. I did not see it, so I cannot tell you how it was made. There was some travelling showmen from Osaka at Sakai. They had a tiger and many curious animals and the stuffed Kudan.

From this excerpt of folklore alone we can see the origins of the kudan, a popular idiom using the creature's name—*kudan no gotoshi*, or like the kudan, meaning that something was an undeniable truth—and stories that travellers used them in exhibitions as they moved around the country.

The idiom *kudan no gotoshi* can actually be traced all the way back to the Heian Period (794-1185). It featured in *The Pillow Book*, written by Sei Shonagon in 1002, and was often used at the end of official documents in Western Japan to signify "as the kudan's promises are never wrong, neither are there falsehoods here." But if the kudan did not exist until the Edo Period, how were they talking about it over 800 years earlier?

It's commonly thought today that the yokai kudan came about as a later creation in response to this phrase. The Chinese character used for the yokai can also mean "passage, paragraph, or the above mentioned." With this in mind, another way of reading *kudan no gotoshi* could mean "as the above mentioned is true, no falsehood is present." Makes a little more sense than a creature that spouts prophecies that didn't even exist at the time, doesn't it?

FIRST SIGHTINGS

The first recorded sighting of a kudan goes all the way back to 1827, on Mount Tateyama in what is now Toyama Prefecture. The creature was called "kudabe" rather than "kudan," and some villagers who were gathering wild plants came across it in the mountains. The creature said to them, "Several years from now, many people will fall victim to a plague. However, those who look upon a picture of myself will be spared." Rumours quickly spread, and people began carrying pictures with them of the kudabe to ward against evil.

The oldest known example of the creature using the name "kudan" comes from 1836, eleven years later. A picture of a cow with a human face was printed on a tile block with the following text:

December 1836, in Tango Province (modern-day Kyoto), Mount Kurahashi, a beast with a human face on a cow's body called the kudan appeared.

The kudan also appeared in December 1705, and afterwards there was an abundant harvest. Any who affix an image of the kudan will see their family become prosperous, avoid illness, and escape from all disasters, finding themselves in a most fruitful year. Truly, what an auspicious beast it is! The kudan is an honest beast, and that is why we write "kudan no gotoshi" at the end of contracts.

During the time this tile block was printed, the Great Tempo Famine was taking place, so it's thought this block was designed in order to lift people's spirits. These were the building blocks for the legend as it's known today.

Towards the end of the Edo Period, stories of kudan became more commonplace. Instead of appearing randomly in the mountains, people's cattle were giving birth to them. In April 1867, a tile block was printed with the title "Kudan Photo." Alongside a picture of a kudan, it stated:

A kudan was born in the countryside of Izumo. It prophecised, "This year will be a bountiful harvest, however, from early autumn an epidemic will come to pass." Three days later, it died. In order to avoid this misfortune, buy this tile and hang it within your house.

Not a bad way for a tile block printer to make some money as the Edo Period was coming to a close.

On June 21, 1909, a Nagoya newspaper printed a story that said 10 years earlier, a kudan was born on a farm in the Goto Islands. 31 days after birth, the creature said, "Japan will go to war with Russia," and then died. The kudan was stuffed and displayed in the Yahiro Musuem in Nagasaki City. The museum has since closed and the whereabouts of the stuffed kudan are unknown.

In 1930, a kudan was supposedly seen in the forests of Kagawa Prefecture. It said, "Soon a large war will break out. You will win, but a plague will spread. However, if you eat azuki rice within three days of hearing this story, and tie a string around your wrist, you will be safe." By 1933, this story had reached Nagano Prefecture, and school children started taking azuki rice to school for lunch. The story had changed, however, and it was no longer the kudan who made the prophecy but a newborn baby with the head of a snake who was enshrined at Suwa Shrine.

In 1943, a kudan was supposedly born to a clog shop in Iwakuni City, Yamaguchi Prefecture. "Around April or May of this year, the war will end," it said. In the spring of 1945, rumours spread through Matsuyama City, Aichi Prefecture, that said, "A kudan was born in Kobe. It said, 'All who hear and believe my story, and then eat azuki ohagi within three days will avoid the air raids.'"

HOW TO STOP ITS PROPHECY?

Imagine, you're out in the back paddock, doing some farm work, when you notice one of the cows is looking at you funny. You walk over and see a newborn calf lying in the dirt. "Aww, how cute!"

you think, until it turns to look up at you and you see a very human face looking back at you. The abomination starts to speak, telling you of a terrifying calamity that's about to come. It then dies. Once you're done wondering "What the actual fu—" you'll probably start to wonder if there's any way to avoid the prophecy from coming true. As it turns out, there is.

Modern versions of the kudan legend suggest that the creature is born in pairs. When a male kudan is born, so is a female. The male is the one who gives prophecies, and in order to escape from what he has proclaimed, you must find the female, wherever she is. Once you find her, she will tell you how to avoid the male's prophecy. Easy enough, right? There can't be that many cows with human faces around. That stuff is likely to make the news…

THE COW WOMAN?

After the Second World War, as Japan began to change and rebuild, stories of the kudan started to change as well. It was no longer just a cow with a human face. Sometimes it was also a woman with a cow's face. She was called *Ushi-onna*, or the Cow Woman. Stories of her are said to be limited to the Mount Rokko area in Hyogo Prefecture. Tales tell of a woman with a cow's head, dressed in a kimono, dancing in the ruins of an air raid shelter and eating the corpses of dead animals. Other versions claim her to be the daughter of Gozu, or Ox-Head, a guardian of the Underworld in Chinese and

Japanese mythology.

Yet, no matter how you look at it, these two legends differ greatly. Kudan is a cow with a human face. Ushi-onna is a woman with a cow's face. Kudan tells prophecies upon birth, and Ushi-onna only speaks when spoken to. The only thing they have in common is their half-human, half-cow nature, and even that is reversed. While their legends may have gotten mixed up over the years, it's important to remember that they are two distinctly different legends. Ushi-onna is not a kudan.

Headless Rider

It's important to pay close attention when you're driving through the heart of Tokyo late at night. When it gets late, the Headless Rider appears, and if the Headless Rider overtakes you, he will cause you to crash and die.

The Headless Rider is a ghost who was attacked by violent street gangs in the past. They tied a piano string across the road which he then drove through, cutting off his head.

To this day he continues searching the roads for his missing head.

ABOUT

Legends of the Headless Rider appear all over Japan, with some of the more common locations being the streets of Tokyo, Okutama City in the west of Tokyo, and Usui Pass on the borders of Gunma and Nagano Prefectures. The Headless Rider is generally considered to be a (former) gang member himself, although in some versions he's an unfortunate soul who happened to be in the wrong place at the wrong time. He spends his afterlife roaming the streets looking for his missing head, and if he overtakes you on the road, it spells your doom shortly thereafter. Stories of headless riders all around the world aren't new, but how did this particular one come about?

HISTORY

There have been stories of headless horse riders and headless warriors since at least the Sengoku Era, but in terms of the modern legend, it's thought that stories of the Headless Rider first spread through Japan in the early 1980s thanks to the Australian movie *Stone*. The film features a scene where a gang member rides his bike through a piece of wire stretched across the road, cutting his head off, exactly like in the legend of today.

The Headless Rider later featured in a special episode of *Gakkou no Kaidan: Headless Rider!! The Curse of Death*, a popular children's show which aired on August 24, 2001. In this version, merely looking at the Headless Rider was enough to ensure your doom. Once seeing him, anything nearby that would be able to sever a head would attack; the environment (and not the rider) doing its best to kill you. This version of the Headless Rider only appeared on the day of his death, however, making him otherwise easy to avoid.

On May 23, 2002, a very real incident that mirrored the film *Stone* took place. At 6:30 in the morning, a 25-year-old man rode his bike into a bookstore parking lot in Akita City, Akita Prefecture. He was on his way to work at a nearby construction lot, but failed to notice the seven millimetre wide, 18 metre long wire that had been placed across the parking lot entrance. The wire severed his head clean off, killing him instantly. The owners of the bookstore reported that gang members were using the parking lot at night, so they placed the wire across the entrance to keep them out. This news brought rumours of the Headless Rider back into people's minds once more and the legend gained new life.

REAL-LIFE SIGHTINGS?

Not long after the Akita incident, people around Japan started claiming they saw real headless riders on the streets. One explanation given for this rise in sightings was black motorcycle helmets. Motorcycle gangs tended not to wear helmets at all, or if they did, they left the face wide open and unprotected. However, when wearing a full black motorcycle helmet at night, it's easy to see how a quick glance at a cyclist passing by might make it appear as though they had no head. People have suggested that some riders even did this on purpose, going out of their way to appear "invisible" on the night streets and taking pleasure in people's reactions to them. The increase of motorcyclists on sports bikes, where the rider leans forward while zooming through the streets, may also have contributed to Headless Rider sightings.

VARIATIONS

On Mount Hiko in Fukuoka Prefecture you can supposedly find an entire gang of Headless Riders roaming the mountain streets. Slight variations of this legend have their heads come flying at you. First you see their bikes, and then in a different location you hear their death screams as the heads come flying. Sometimes the heads are still wearing helmets, sometimes they're not.

Another version of the tale tells of a couple on a bike ride late at night. The woman, sitting behind the man, appears to be enjoying the high speeds and so, in an effort to please her, the man drives even faster. However, when they turn a corner, he notices a bent sign sticking out across the road. He screams to warn the woman of danger and ducks, narrowly escaping with his life. It's not until he stops at the next traffic light and looks back to see if the woman is okay that he realises she's missing her head. Some versions elaborate and claim that when the man returns to the bent sign, a voice from a severed head calls out to him, "Don't leave me here."

Another Headless Rider exists in Ikebukuro. Tales tell of a rider near the Sunshine 60 building who was decapitated by a falling piece of metal from a truck in front of him. The bike continued riding for several minutes after the rider lost his head, finally colliding with a guardrail. The rider's ghost continues to haunt the area after death, looking for his missing head.

Some versions feature the Headless Rider not looking for his head, but for the gang members that killed him. These criminals also tied a piano string across the road, which killed the rider, and then fled in a white car. If you happen to pass by that same spot in a white car, the ghost of the rider will appear, looking for those who took his life.

You can also find tales told of community members troubled by noisy bike gangs late at night. In order to deal with the constant disturbances, the residents tied a rope across the street which ended up killing one of the riders.

No matter how or where he was created, the Headless Rider's legacy is sure to live on for quite some time. People do love a tragic and terrifying story, after all.

Sadako's Phone Number

090-4444-4444.

They say that if you ring this unlucky number, you'll get through to Sadako. Try it for yourself. You'll hear a strange sound, like "boooooooooooooooo."

However, be careful. All who call this number will meet with a horrific accident within seven days.

ABOUT

Ring by Suzuki Koji was first published in 1991, although it wasn't until the film version was released in 1998 that Sadako really hit the big time. Sadako should need no introduction, but part of her curse in the film involves dying a week after watching her tape. Here we can see her week-long curse at work again. Call this number and instead of Sadako calling you, you'll get straight through to her, and then you'll die within the week.

How is this Sadako's number? Those of you with some familiarity of the Japanese language will likely have recognised why immediately. The number "4" can be pronounced "*shi*" in Japanese, which is also the same word for "death." For that reason, 4 is considered to be an unlucky number in Japan. 090-4444-4444. Yeah, there's no denying that's a cursed number at first sight.

This legend has been around at least as long as the movie has. There are records of people talking about the number online as far back as 2000, and even then it wasn't an unknown legend. Much like the tale states, people who called the number got a strange beeping sound in return, confirming its creepy nature. "But did they die?" I hear you asking. Probably not, because as I'm sure you guessed, it's not really Sadako's phone number. Sadako doesn't exist (or is that just what she wants you to believe?).

THE TRUTH

In reality, the phone number belonged to the phone company au. It was a transmission line, which was why people got the strange long beep when they called it. At present, the number is no longer in use, presumably because so many people kept calling it trying to get through to Sadako.

Interestingly, and perhaps as a good sign of humour, if you type the number into the jpnumber website, a database of phone numbers in Japan, the listing comes up with "Sadako's Phone Number" in the business name section. The number itself is still owned by au's parent company KDDI, and a quick glance through the list of recent comments shows that people are still calling the number to this day. Some even claim that they hear a groaning voice on the other end. If you want to call and check for yourself, you can; it *is* a real phone number. That part's not a legend. You're sadly not likely to hear much on the other end though; it is, fittingly, a dead number after all.

The fact that no-one has taken this number and used it for marketing purposes still astounds me, to be honest.

Blue Crayon

A married couple bought an old house out in the suburbs. The house was close to the station, there were plenty of supermarkets around, and it received a lot of sunlight. Not only that, but it was incredibly cheap as well. It was perfect.

A friend help them move in, and then they drank late into the night. It was too late to go home, so the friend stayed the night with them in their new house.

That night they heard what sounded like a child's footsteps running down the hall, waking them up. They decided they must have been imagining things and went back to bed, but this time they were woken up by the sound of a child talking. By the time morning came, not a single one of them had gotten any sleep.

They found the previous night's events to be strange. Too strange. Something had to be wrong with the house. They investigated the hallway and discovered a discarded blue crayon. Of course, it didn't belong to either the couple or their friend.

Then they realised something. The layout of the house seemed off. The area they found the crayon in was the end of the hall, but according to the house plans, there was enough space behind it to fit another room.

They knocked on the wall. It sounded like there was an empty space behind it. They tore the wallpaper off and discovered a door. Nervously, they opened it and prepared themselves for something they might not want to see…

…But there was nothing there. It was just an empty room, its walls covered in something written in blue crayon.

Father mother I'm sorry please let me out.
Father mother I'm sorry please let me out.
Father mother I'm sorry please let me out.
Father mother I'm sorry please let me out.
Father mother I'm sorry please let me out.
Father mother I'm sorry please let me out.
Father mother I'm sorry please let me out.

ABOUT

This urban legend has been around since the late 1980s. It's also known as "Red Crayon" with slight variations, but the gist of the story remains the same. A couple buys a house that seems too good to be true, they hear strange things in the night, they discover a crayon on the floor and realise the layout of the house is strange, whereupon they discover a hidden room that is covered in crayon, the message of a poor child screaming for help.

Comedian Ijuin Hikaru shared this story in 1997 on an episode of the variety show *Yamada Kuniko no Shiawase ni Shite yo*. From there it spread to the masses and took off in popularity. One viewer of the show claimed the story was their personal experience that they had submitted to a magazine, and soon people began to spread the story as something real that happened to a friend of a friend, cementing its urban legend status. In the end, nobody was able to discover who really created the story, and Ijuin admitted that he heard the story from a work colleague where it was already being treated as an urban legend.

INSPIRED WORKS

A similar story was shared on 2chan on August 11, 2000. This story purported to be a true experience the poster's friend had while working in real estate. The real estate agent noticed that one particular apartment had a hallway that was shorter than the rest and, after getting permission, knocked the wall down to discover a small closet-like space had been created. The inside walls were covered in red crayon, this time saying "*mother mother mother mother mother.*"

In 2012, a Vocaloid song was released called "Crayon" that featured lyrics about being in an enclosed space and "please let me out" repeated several times. Many listeners pointed out that this song was likely based on the blue crayon legend.

The story is still commonly shared today and widely regarded as a *kaidan* classic.

Daddy's Back

There was a married couple who detested each other. Their relationship had long chilled, and they argued every day. Even so, the one thing that kept them from divorcing was their young son, an only child.

However, the father finally reached breaking point and murdered the mother. He disposed of the body and told everyone that she had gone back home to stay with her family. The father soon noticed something strange though. Their son never seemed sad that his mother was gone, nor did he cry out for her.

One day he decided to ask the boy about it.

"Hey, don't you feel sad that your mother hasn't been around lately?"

"No, I'm not sad. Mummy's still here."

"Huh? Where is she?"

"She's been on Daddy's back this whole time."

ABOUT

This story also goes by the name "Sixth Sense" or "Piggy Back" and is considered a *kaidan* classic. It's often used as the basis for other stories and has appeared on variety shows and radio programs numerous times over the years. There's little information about when it first came to be, but it's been around for several decades at least. It's often retold with minor variations, but the punchline always remains the same: Mummy never went anywhere, she's been clinging to Daddy (as a vengeful spirit) the whole time.

There is a phrase in Japanese that goes "*nana-sai made wa kami no uchi.*" It means that until a child turns seven, they belong to the gods. As in other cultures, childhood was a tumultuous time in ancient Japan and many died before reaching adulthood. If a child died, it was thought they were returning to the gods. This brought about the idea that young children were close to divinity, and they were therefore able to see things adults couldn't. This young boy, inhabiting the precarious region between humanity and divinity, isn't sad because his dead mother isn't gone; not to him, anyway. Daddy, no longer being a small child blessed with the gift of seeing the other side, has no idea that she's been haunting him all this time, and if you're anything like me, that's a terrifying thought.

The Knock

A, her boyfriend B, and their two friends C and D decided to go on a mountain climbing trip to celebrate graduating university. The four friends were from the same club and had been friends since they started university.

They planned to set out for the cabin on the first day by car, spend the night there, and then go mountain climbing the next day. They wanted to go together, but B had an interview for a new job, so everyone else went by car and he would join them after on his bike.

A sat in the back while D drove, and his girlfriend C sat in the passenger's seat. They were making good progress, but on the way up the mountain things suddenly turned chilly. Perhaps it was because of the rain the day before, but there was a slight fog hanging over the area as well.

At first, A was excited as she chatted with her friends, but she soon became drowsy and then fell asleep. When she opened her eyes, they were near the cabin. A realised she must have slept for quite some time. She got out of the car, her body stiff and lethargic. She breathed in the cool air, and looking around at the misty mountains, she noticed C and D looked concerned.

"What's wrong?" A whispered.

The pair suddenly turned around and then locked eyes with each other. An uncomfortable silence descended, and A wondered if they had forgotten the cabin key.

"Hey, did something happen?"

The couple exchanged glances and finally nodded.

"A, keep calm and listen closely, okay?"

"You see, we got a call from the police just before. B was on his way here by bike and… He road over the edge of the mountain and died."

"N-No…"

A was at a loss for words and fell to her knees. Even after they entered the cabin, A remained dumbfounded and in shock. She sat on the couch hugging her knees tight.

Night soon fell. Suddenly, there was a loud knock at the cabin door.

"Hey! A! It's me! Open up!"

It was B's voice! A jumped up to open the door, but C and D pulled her back and restrained her.

"You can't! B's dead! It must be his ghost! He came to take you with him! You mustn't open the door!"

"That's right, A! Stay with us!"

The pair harshly warned A against opening the door, but the knocking continued.

"A, come on, open up! Please! You're in there, aren't you? Open the door, please!" B screamed desperately.

She wanted to see him again. Just one more time. That was all A could think. She shook C and D off and ran for the door. The door her boyfriend was waiting behind.

She flung the door open and was greeted with a white roof. B, his eyes swollen and bloodshot, looked down at her.

"A… Thank god…"

B grabbed her hand and grasped it tightly within his own. A couldn't understand what was going on, so B explained. There was an accident, but it was A, C, and D who drove over the edge of a cliff. A was thrown from the backseat, and she had been stuck in a state between life and death all night long.

"C and D died instantly," B said, hugging her tightly. "They must have been lonely there all by themselves, so they wanted to take you along with them."

ABOUT

This is another story that's been doing the rounds since at least the late 1990s. There are several variations on the story, such as how many people are involved and where the story takes place, but the general theme remains the same across them all. There is an accident, a woman is warned not to open the door because her boyfriend is dead, but in the end she gives in and it turns out that everyone else was dead, and they were trying to take her into the afterlife with them. It was her boyfriend's knocking on the door that brought her back to the living. This story featured in an episode of the variety show *Yonimo Kimyo na Monogatari*, and has appeared in several manga set pieces as well.

VARIATIONS

On August 5, 2000, a slightly different version of this legend was shared on 2chan. This one, called "You Are!" tells the tale of two couples who go to the beach instead of the mountains. They decide to have a race on the way back, with one young man (B) on his bike while the rest drive back by car. Of course, B never makes it, and the other couple are forced to tell his girlfriend (A) that he had an accident while they were racing and he died. After he died, however, they heard him banging on their door and calling for them to open up, so if he does the same thing to her, she mustn't open the door under any circumstances. The rest of the story runs much the same way, and eventually A caves in, opens the door, and finds herself in a hospital room. Turns out the others were the dead ones all along.

Another variation of this story features in Inagawa Junji's book *Inagawa Junji no Sugoku Kowai Hanashi Best Selection*, released in 2001. Inagawa Junji is famous for his retellings of ghost stories, so when he shares a story it quickly becomes popular. In Inagawa's version, called "The Messenger of Death," a young woman and two men from the same club at university go to stay in a cabin in the mountains. In this version, the woman is dating one of the men (A) while the other (C) has a secret crush on her.

The two men leave the woman behind to go shopping; however, only C returns. He informs her that they were just in an accident and A died. If he happens to return, she must not open the door under any circumstances. Of course, A eventually returns and starts knocking loudly on the door, asking his girlfriend to open up. The woman can't help herself because she loves him and opens the door. It turns out that, surprise surprise, C was actually the dead one all along.

Japanese culture, and particularly its horror stories, are most at home in the ghost, or *yurei* genre, which makes stories like this one and its terrifying twist at the end so popular and long-lasting.

Running Ghost

The students of Dorm H at a university in T City, Ibaraki Prefecture, have recently been troubled by something. That something is a ghost.

The ghost looks like a marathon runner and runs from one end of the dorms to the other, going straight through the walls. People have taken to calling it the "Running Ghost." It treads on students as it runs through the dorm, and many wake up in surprise at being stepped on.

"Come to think of it, wasn't there a member of the track team who died right before reaching the finishing line of a marathon? That's gotta be him."

After hearing the above, one student had an idea. The next night, everyone gathered in his room. He prepared a finish line and everyone held ribbons to cheer. Then, finally, the late night running ghost appeared. The ghost slipped through the wall as usual, and when the students cut the tape, the ghost appeared satisfied and disappeared.

When some of the students asked why the ghost had disappeared, the young man who came up with the idea answered, "What are you saying? He died before reaching the finishing line, right? That's why we cut the tape for him. That was the goal tape he never got to reach while alive."

ABOUT

The university in question is Tsukuba University in Ibaraki Prefecture. Dorm H refers to Hirasuna Dorm, one of several dorms used by Tsukuba students. Tsukuba University has a wide variety of urban legends surrounding it, but this is one of the more famous ones. Ironically, while this legend is well known to those outside of the university, many students claim to have never heard it before.

It's unclear where this legend originated from. Some have surmised that the story was originally a regular ghost tale that became so popular it was placed in Tsukuba University to give it authenticity. The university already has a bunch of other legends, so what's one more to the mix?

There's also an interesting after story which mentions someone from the dorms accidentally saying, "Ready, go!" which causes the running ghost to appear again. At least they know how to deal with him this time…

Middle of the Photo

When taking a photo with three people, you must not sit in the middle. Whoever is in the middle when a photo is taken will meet with misfortune, and in some cases, death.

ABOUT

This rather short urban legend gets straight to the point, but never says why being the middle person in a three-person photo is dangerous. Some have suggested this legend came about because traditionally, the eldest and most respected person would sit in the middle for a photo, signifying their position of power. Being the eldest also meant that they were probably the person with the least amount of time left to live, and the person most likely to see their health start failing soon. Whether this is true or not, the idea of the middle being a precarious position prevailed and the legend persists in modern times.

ORIGINS

The origins of this legend can be traced back even further, however. As in many other countries, superstitions about photos have been around for many years. The first camera arrived in Japan on a Dutch ship in 1848, and taking portraits soon became a popular pastime. These cameras were large square boxes, however, and the image of a tiny person floating inside made people suspect that these magical boxes were actually capturing people's souls.

Rumours quickly spread that "taking a photo will steal your soul!" This was especially dangerous for the person in the centre of the photo, the one directly in the camera's sights. Old photographs were of questionable quality compared to today's standards, and often the person in the middle was the only one in focus. This led to photos where the person in the centre was perfectly clear, yet the people beside them were blurry. This could only mean one thing: the person in the middle's soul was taken from them, thus producing a clearer image than anyone else.

As a result, many people tried to avoid taking photos in threes, and if for some reason a photo absolutely had to be taken, some photographers went so far as to include a stuffed toy or doll to take the number of "people" in the photo up to four.

Similar to the reason given above, to take a photo in the Edo Period required going to a photo studio and spending a lot of money to do so. This meant that photos were, in general, limited to the wealthy. The most senior person would take the centre position as a sign of respect, and being the most senior person meant there was a higher chance of them passing away due to old age first.

Modern cameras, of course, are able to focus on several faces at once and reproduce all of them in perfectly clear quality, and very few people believe the camera actually steals your soul anymore. And yet the legend remains, and you'll still find people today who refuse to stand in the middle of a three-shot photo, particularly amongst the elderly.

Red Scarf

A young girl with a red scarf transferred to a new elementary school. One day, a boy in her class asked her, "Why are you always wearing that scarf?"

"When you start junior high, I'll tell you then," she answered.

Both the boy and the girl went to the same junior high school. One day the boy asked her, "We're in junior high now, so tell me, why do you always wear that scarf?"

"If you go to the same high school as me, I'll tell you then," the girl replied.

The pair ended up going to the same high school together.

"Tell me, why are you always wearing that red scarf?" the boy asked her again.

"If you go to the same university as me, I'll tell you then," the girl replied with a shy laugh.

The pair entered the same university. They started dating, and eventually got married. Shortly after they got married, the boy asked her, "By the way, why are you always wearing that scarf?"

"Do you really want to know?" the girl asked, her eyes downcast.

"We're married, aren't we? Surely you can tell me now."

"Okay, fine. I'll tell you…"

The girl finally took off the scarf she always wore.

"If you hadn't asked, we could have been together forever…"

Bang!

The girl's head fell to the floor. The scarf had been the only thing keeping her head on…

ABOUT

This legend first started to spread in the mid-1990s and was especially popular with junior and high school students. It's both scary and heartbreaking, a winning combination for many in the throes of puberty. As the internet became more popular in the early 2000s, the story spread even further, and additions were made to the ending as it was shared around. One new ending added the following:

> "Well, how about we get you a scarf that matches as well?"
>
> Even now, the girl with the red scarf and the boy with the blue scarf are living happily together in that household.

Yet another embellishment went even further:

> Word has it that recently, they've given birth to a baby with a purple scarf as well.

The story draws several parallels with older classics, such as *Yuki-onna* and *Tsuru no Ongaeshi*. In both of these classic tales, the woman is hiding a secret; in *Yuki-onna*'s case, the fact that she's Yuki-onna, and in *Tsuru no Ongaeshi*'s case, the fact that the man's wife is really a bird. When the man persists with knowing what the secret is, she is forced to reveal her true nature and the relationship ends. The newer additions to this urban legend attempt to add a happy ending and avoid that fate, but they don't exist in the original, which is truer to the classics.

The girl is also somewhat reminiscent of the yokai rokurokubi, a woman who can elongate her neck or even detach her head completely, and hitouban, a yokai based on a Chinese legend that can do the same. In rare variations of the legend, the girl is actually revealed to be a hitouban, but in general there's no reason given as to why her head is being kept on by a scarf. It's scarier that way.

Turbo Granny

A man was driving through the mountains late one night. Before long he heard a sound coming from behind him. He looked in the rear-view mirror, thinking it might be another car approaching him, but there was no light. He must have been imagining it, he thought, and continued driving.

Bang! Bang!

The next moment, something hit the window. Surprised, the man turned and saw an old lady running beside the car, grinning at him. The old lady took off, out-speeding the car. A short while later the man crashed and died.

ABOUT

Turbo Granny, or Jet Granny, is perhaps the most famous of all "granny" legends. There are numerous variations on her name, where she appears, and what exactly happens if you see her, but the one consistent factor across all stories is her incredible speed. She's said to be able to reach over 140 kilometres per hour. Not really someone you want to run into late at night on the mountain roads!

Although Turbo Granny is considered a modern yokai, it's thought that she's simply a new variation on an old tale called "*Ushiro wo Furimukeba*" (If You Turn Around). Danger in most horror situations tends to come from our blind spots, and we're unable to see what's behind us unless we turn around. It's that old cliche of "phew, nothing's there, it was all my imagination…" and then you turn to the side and whoops, it wasn't my imagination after all. Something *is* there, and it's unexpected and terrifying. In this case, the last thing you would expect to see while driving along a mountain road late at night would be an old lady keeping up with your car.

PARTICULARS

Turbo Granny's traditional haunt was Rokkosan in Hyogo Prefecture, but as her fame grew, so did sightings of her all over the country. In early stories, Turbo Granny was a harmless yokai. She simply appeared running beside your car, grinned, and then ran off. Perhaps the look of surprise on drivers' faces was enough for her, or perhaps she was just getting some exercise. Who knows? But as her legend grew, so did her danger. A scary story in which the monster causes no harm isn't all that scary after a while, so Turbo Granny became more threatening. Now, if you saw her and she overtook you, that meant you would crash and die. Supposedly this was because your body went into shock upon seeing her and would refuse to move. Not the best situation to be in when driving through Japan's perilous mountains.

Once a harmless and even somewhat charming yokai, stories of Turbo Granny's reign of terror on the roads soon spread through television and manga. She became less of a joke and more of a serious legend, the living embodiment of that blind spot behind us all where danger lurks unseen. Seeing her was no longer something you could joke about with friends; seeing her meant certain death.

VARIATIONS

Turbo Granny doesn't roam the dark streets of Japan alone; she has numerous old folk helping her out. Here are a few buddies who are believed to be derived from her original story:

- Basketball Granny: likes to dribble a basketball while chasing bikes on the road. She then throws the ball to unsuspecting riders. If they catch the ball, their bike will crash and they'll die. If they ignore the ball, the ball will hit them in the head, causing them to crash and die. There's no winning either way. Also known as Dribbling Granny thanks to her hot basketball skills.
- Coffin Granny: likes to chase drivers, grab them, shove them in a coffin and then cremate them alive.
- Bonnet Granny: likes to jump onto the bonnets of cars driving along the highway. This is in an attempt to make drivers swerve and crash, but if you can manage to drive another seven kilometres with her on the front of your car, she'll eventually leave you alone.
- Elbow Granny: likes to chase cars on her elbows. There's a good reason for this: like Teketeke, Elbow Granny has no legs. If she manages to catch you, it's game over.
- Hopping Granny: likes to land in front of

cars on mountain roads, causing them to freak out and slam on the breaks. She jumps out of the way before they can hit her, but this usually results in the car going over the edge of a cliff and the driver dying.
- Jumping Granny: likes to jump incredible distances, just like Hopping Granny. We'll be looking at her a little more in-depth later.

Aside from her old lady friends, plenty of other speedy folks are said to haunt Japan's roads as well:

- Highway Businessman: a man in a suit who chases down cars on highways.
- Bike Office Lady: the company worker who chases down cars on her old-fashioned Japanese motorcycle.
- Hand Cart Woman: a lady in Hokkaido who pulls a hand cart and races cars with it, reaching speeds of up to 80 kilometres per hour.
- Crawling Woman: a woman in white who haunts mountain roads and crawls behind cars on all fours at incredible speed.
- Missile Girl: the high school girl who rides a missile.
- Skipping Girl: a young girl near the Tsuyama Interchange in Okayama who wears a white blouse, red skirt, backpack and skips between cars at speeds of 80 kilometres per hour.
- Handball Mari-chan: the spirit of a girl who was killed in a hit-and-run accident while

playing with a Japanese handball.

- Handball Grandpa: an old man who chases down cars while playing with a Japanese handball.
- Crawling Baby: crawls with incredible speed alongside cars on the highway.

Beware if ever driving Japan's streets, particularly at night. Turbo Granny and her friends are seemingly everywhere.

Jumping Granny

A young man arrived at a cemetery in Nagoya to test his courage with a group of friends. The cemetery was creepy at night, which made the group even more excited. They decided to circle around the area.

Shortly after they started walking, they heard a sound. They turned to see what it was. Endless tombstones lined the park, but something strange stood out amongst them.

There was an old woman wearing *geta* (Japanese wooden clogs), jumping from tombstone to tombstone, over incredible distances not possible by any normal human.

ABOUT

A group of YouTubers looked up what urban legends were popular in Nagoya and the first thing that popped up was “Jumping Granny.” According to the legends, this “Jumping Granny” only appears in Aichi Prefecture, specifically in the capital of Nagoya, so they wanted to know how well-known she was, and what information they could discover about her from the general public. They stopped random people in the street to ask them about her and roughly half had no idea who she was. All of these people grew up outside of Nagoya, which confirmed their suspicions that she was unknown outside the local area. Of those who had heard of her, the responses were varied. Nobody seemed to know exactly who she was, what she did, or where she appeared. But she could jump really high. Everyone agreed on that.

By all accounts, Jumping Granny appears to be a recent urban legend that began sometime during the last few years. She's closely tied to Yagoto Cemetery, one of the largest cemeteries in Nagoya, and Heiwa Park a few kilometres away. Supposedly she can jump anywhere from four to 10 metres, and not just on tombstones. Some stories have her lurking in the woods and jumping to the top of trees, while others see her on highways jumping all over the place and causing drivers to crash.

On an interesting side note, there is also a "Rolling Grandpa" that roams the streets of Nagoya at night. Much like the granny he's no doubt based on, he chases people at high speed, only this grandpa rolls instead of jumps. There's also a "Hopping Granny" who may or may not be another name for the Jumping Granny, although she's often linked to Turbo Granny as well. She seems to occupy a middle ground between the two.

With Japan's ageing population, it shouldn't be too much of a surprise to see scary old folk stories on the rise, and I suspect we'll see even more of them in the future.

564219

A high school girl received a strange number on her pager. It said "564219." The girl had no idea what it meant. Then it came again. "564219."

A few days later, the girl was killed. Everyone, if you happen to receive the numbers "564219" (*ko ro shi ni i ku*), take care. You could be next.

ABOUT

As you can tell by the use of a pager in this legend, it's rather old. The meaning behind it may not be immediately apparent to an English speaker, but that's because the "warning" is hidden in the Japanese pronunciation of the numbers involved.

Japanese numbers often have several ways they can be pronounced depending on the situation. In this legend it's literally spelt out afterwards, just in case people weren't quick on the uptake: 5 (*ko*) 6 (*ro*) 4 (*shi*) 2 (*ni*) 1 (*i*) 9 (*ku*). This spells out *koroshi ni iku*, which in English translates to "I'm going to kill you." Straight forward, yet still sneaky enough to inspire fear once somebody realises the hidden meaning.

Few people carry pagers anymore, and high school girls these days probably wouldn't even know what a pager was if it landed on their desk, so more recent versions of this legend have changed it to a phone number you can call instead. It should be clear at first glance that 564219 isn't enough numbers to be a phone number, but that's its charm. It's a special number that will forward you to a *shinigami*, a god of death, and that shinigami will come to kill you for calling them direct:

> If you call the number 564219, you'll be put through to a shinigami who will come to collect your soul. Whether it's actually true or not is up for debate, but it's not something you should mess around with lightly.

While the method of receiving or calling this number may change with technology, the heart of this legend is likely to be around for a while. People do love a deadly pun, after all.

Tripping Over a Tombstone

Graveyards are said to be unlucky places, and if you happen to trip over a tombstone, they say that the dead will reach out to claim your leg. In order to avoid this, you must leave your shoe behind on the grave instead.

ABOUT

Parents often tell their children this legend, or at least some variation where it's mortally dangerous to trip over a tombstone. For example, the following is a tale commonly told in the countryside:

> A group of five friends were playing in a graveyard after school. One of the boys tripped over a tombstone and the others told him, "If you fall over in a graveyard, you have to leave one leg behind."
>
> Of course, the boy couldn't cut his own leg off, so he left a shoe instead. A few days later, the five were playing at the same graveyard again, only this time, one of the boys tripped and took two of his friends down with him like dominoes.
>
> "We need to leave a shoe behind!" they said again. Two of the boys removed a shoe and placed it on the ground, but the other boy refused. His shoes were brand new and his favourite. He didn't want to leave one behind.
>
> "If you don't leave one, they'll come and take your leg," the boys told him, but in the end he

left with both his shoes on. Nobody thought much of it, but on the way home one boy was nearly hit by a truck, and another narrowly avoided being crushed by fallen materials at a construction site.

The next day, the boys told each other about what happened on their way home. "It's the graveyard curse!" they screamed. They wondered what happened to their friend who didn't leave his shoe behind, but he didn't come to school that day. The following day their teacher suddenly announced that he had transferred schools.

In reality, that same day the boy refused to leave his shoe behind, he was overcome with sudden paralysis on the right side of his body and never recovered…

Losing a leg (or suffering paralysis) isn't the only thing to fear if you happen to accidentally trip over a tombstone. Other stories claim that if you fall over, that wound will never heal. If you fall over, your life will be shortened. If you fall over, you'll be spirited away. If you fall over, your spirit will escape. If you fall over, you must change your name. If you fall over, you'll become a cat (yes, seriously…). There are all sorts of variations from different areas of Japan, all designed to keep rambunctious children from desecrating grave sites. Aside from the obvious reason of not wanting children to run wild in a graveyard, how did this legend come to be?

ORIGINS

It's thought this superstition came about as a way to teach children of the hidden dangers in graveyards. At present, 99.9% of bodies are cremated after death in Japan, but before World War II, most were buried. Some local governments now ban burials altogether, but many rural areas retain their old traditions. It wasn't uncommon in the early Showa Period for these bodies to ferment and produce gases that burst forth through the ground, opening small holes and cracks above them. This made it easy for people to unknowingly fall into one and trip over.

Children often used graveyards as playgrounds at the time, and aside from the sudden holes in the ground, they were also faced with sharp, pointed tombstones and the possibility that knocking one over would crush them. Thus, to keep their children safe, parents told them that falling over in a graveyard was not only unlucky, but it would lead to death if they were not careful, and a superstition was born.

What about the shoe? Well, if you've upset a spirit by tripping over its grave, the least you can do is leave something behind so they don't come and take something—like your leg—for themselves…

On an interesting side note, buying burial plots in modern Japan is now so expensive that "grave apartments" have started to spring up around the country. Here you can buy a small plot within a much larger crypt to keep your family's remains for a price many times cheaper than a regular burial plot. No news yet on whether the *yurei* in these grave apartments are constantly complaining about their neighbours' noise, but you never know…

Exclamation Point Road Sign

Have you ever seen a yellow road sign with a black exclamation point on it before? According to the Road Traffic Law, if you see one of these signs it signifies "other dangers." Underneath the exclamation point the sign should list what danger it is: for example, weak gravel by the side of the road, a sudden steep incline, and so on. In order to understand what the particular danger is, you must read what is written underneath the exclamation point.

However, there are some signs that don't include this information. They only have an exclamation point and nothing else. In reality, these signs are placed where ghosts have been seen, and so they serve as a warning to all that ghosts are nearby. The Ministry of Transport is unable to officially acknowledge the presence of ghosts and the danger they pose to the public, so they place exclamation point signs in dangerous areas to let the public know.

ABOUT

Signs featuring exclamation marks are used all over the world and generally mean "other dangers," like they do in this legend. The "other danger" is usually specified in text underneath the sign, but sometimes in Japan you might come across a sign that is just an exclamation point and nothing else, or otherwise just says "warning" beneath it. In that case, what is the danger? If you believe this urban legend, it's ghosts!

It's not difficult to see how some people may have come to this conclusion. The signs are supposed to specify what the danger is so you can avoid it. If it says beware ice, you can drive more slowly. If it says steep slope, you can prepare yourself for a sudden uphill drive. But if the sign is empty or just says "warning," what am I supposed to be wary of? Japan has a long and rich history of *yurei*, so it doesn't take much of a push to think that might be the reason why.

Rumours of these signs are particularly prevalent around Aoyama Cemetery in Tokyo. Numerous urban legends exist regarding the area, but this one states that these signs mysteriously appear and disappear throughout the park. If you happen to run into one, you need to get out of there right away, because it means dangerous ghosts are nearby.

THE TRUTH

Never fear, however. There is an easier and less haunted answer at hand. The reason these signs without warnings exist is very simple: the warnings are too long. Sometimes there might be a lot of trees growing by the side of the road that jut out at dangerous angles, making it difficult to see around corners and, especially in the dark, playing tricks on people's minds. It's a little difficult to explain all that in just a few letters, and so they write nothing at all. They place a general warning sign, which means you should be extra careful about all of your surroundings after that point.

Probably a good idea to always be wary of ghosts on Japanese roads though. Just in case.

Gomiko-san

In the mountains of N Prefecture there exists a woman named Gomiko-san. She roams the mountains late at night, and if you happen to run into her, she will scream, "Don't throw me out!" She'll then cut you into pieces, throw your remains in a trash bag, and then dispose of you.

ABOUT

Gomiko-san first appeared on the internet in the early 2000s, and all we know of her is what's stated in the legend. Where she's from is left vague on purpose, but considering it starts with N, it can only be Niigata, Nagano, Nara, or Nagasaki. These prefectures are spread out across most of Japan, so she could be anywhere (and isn't that the charm of urban legends?), although many internet users place her in either Niigata or Nagano.

It may not be immediately apparent to English speakers, but Gomiko-san's name is a pun on her M.O. *Gomi* means rubbish and *ko* is a common suffix for girls' names. She is literally "Trash Woman," and she disposes of people by cutting them up, putting them in a rubbish bag, and then throwing them away.

Later additions make it supposedly impossible to run away from her unless, if you're in a group, you split up and run in different directions. This will leave one person subject to certain murder and trash disposal while the others escape; presumably to live the rest of their lives with the knowledge that they abandoned their friend to an actual Trash Woman in the mountains.

Interestingly, Gomiko-san features in the movie *Noroi no Gotochi Toshi Densetsu~Hokkaido/Tohoku Hen~* as an urban legend from Hokkaido. The movie came out in 2011 and gives no explanation as to why Gomiko-san is suddenly a Hokkaido legend when she very specifically comes from a prefecture that starts with "N." Still, if you wish to watch a found footage film of people getting cut up and placed in trash bags, Gomiko-san has you covered.

Watching Woman

A student injured himself and was taken to hospital. Thankfully, the injury was only minor, and he was told he would be out of the hospital before the week was up. However, the hospital he was staying in was said to be haunted. The boy didn't believe in ghosts, so even when his friends told him about it, he paid it no mind.

Late one night, the boy woke up and needed to go to the toilet. The hospital seemed creepy at night, but he stumbled over to the toilet anyway. He stood in front of the door and heard something.

Rattle... rattle rattle...

Something metallic was echoing down the end of the hallway.

"What's that? Surgical tools on a trolley? There isn't even a surgery room on this floor..."

The sound slowly got closer. As he suspected, a nurse pushing surgical tools on a trolley soon appeared. But the woman's white robe was covered in blood, and the boy quickly realised that she wasn't human.

He was dumbfounded. If he didn't do something soon, she would find him and it would all be over! But he was injured, so he couldn't move very fast. He squeezed into the toilet and locked the door behind him.

Rattle... Rattle rattle... Squeak...

The sound of the trolley got louder. The boy held his breath and waited for the trolley to pass. As though his wish had been granted, the sound of the trolley soon disappeared.

"Thank god, I'm saved…"

Relieved, the boy went to return to his room. He looked up and locked eyes with the blood-stained nurse. She had noticed him after all. She was hanging over the top of the toilet door, looking down at him all along.

ABOUT

This is a fairly typical Japanese ghost story. You've no doubt seen scenes similar to it in numerous movies over the years. Somebody hears a noise, they try to hide, think they're safe, then they look up and realise the ghost was looking down at them all along. It's terrifying to think about, and that's what makes it such a good scene.

VARIATIONS

A nurse in a hospital isn't the only variation of this story, however. Another less common but still popular version places the story in an old shrine:

> A student went to visit a shrine late one night to test his courage. The shrine was said to be haunted, but the boy wasn't afraid of anything and didn't believe in ghosts to begin with. He was a proud boy, so he went by himself.
>
> He wandered around the empty shrine grounds, but nothing happened. There were no ghosts, no shadows; nothing.
>
> "Of course there's nothing here…" he muttered, when suddenly he heard a noise

coming from the trees behind the shrine. The noise drew his attention, and as his heart beat wildly in his chest, he pushed his way through the branches. Then he saw it. A woman in white clothing was hammering a straw doll to a tree.

Bang! Bang!

The straw doll was stuck to the tree with long nails.

“Ah!” The boy let out a scream before he could stop himself. The girl stopped hammering and turned to look at him, the expression on her face ghastly.

The boy took off running, the girl hot on his heels. He ran as fast as he could, but the girl seemed more familiar with the area than he was, and she soon closed the distance.

“Hihihihihihi!” the woman screamed behind him.

‘She’s gonna get me!’ the boy thought, and then he saw some public toilets not too far ahead. He ran inside, hid himself in the end stall and locked the door. Holding his breath, he listened as stillness fell over the area. He could hear the girl’s footsteps outside, but then they disappeared.

“I’m safe…”

But he couldn’t be too sure of that. The girl might still have been outside. Filled with relief that he could no longer hear the girl’s footsteps, the boy fell asleep inside the stall.

When the boy woke up, he looked at his watch and saw it said 4 a.m.

“It should be okay now.”

He stood up and got ready to leave, but something on the ceiling caught his eye. He looked up and saw the girl in white clothes looking down at him, grinning.

She had been there the whole night.

ORIGINS

Neither the nurse nor the girl at the shrine are thought to be the original versions of this tale. The origins go back much further, to at least the 1960s and feature not a ghost, but a tengu.

In this version, a man hears the sound of *geta* (wooden Japanese clogs) and hides in a toilet until they pass. When he's certain the owner of the sound is gone, he looks up and sees a tengu hanging upside down from the roof, looking at him. Tengu are often depicted wearing geta and can be quite the vicious creatures when they want to be. In the modern day, however, tengu aren't as feared as they once used to be. Thanks to the focus on *yurei* in horror media, most people are more afraid of ghosts than yokai. As such, over time the tengu was replaced with a variety of ghosts in different situations, with the nurse in the hospital being the most common story passed around today.

Red Hanten

A high school girl was in the toilet when she heard something.

"Shall I dress you in a red *hanten* (traditional vest)?"

Rumours of the strange voice soon spread, and it became the talk of the school. Some students even refused to go to the toilets afterwards.

Troubled, the school called the police in to investigate. A strong-willed female officer agreed to go in and have a look; they were the female toilets, after all.

Suddenly, the officers waiting outside heard a voice.

"Dress me in it if you can!"

This was shortly followed by a scream. The officers rushed into the toilet and found it covered in blood, while the unfortunate female officer was lying on the ground like she was wearing a red hanten vest.

ABOUT

By now you should realise that if anybody asks if you would like something in a Japanese toilet, it won't end well. This legend probably brings to mind Aka Manto (who you can find in *Toshiden Vol. 1*), the mysterious figure who haunts school toilets and asks people if they would like red or blue paper.

It turns out that this story actually came from a listener on a radio show that Inagawa Junji, the famous ghost storyteller, worked on. Inagawa told the story in 1986, although the story itself was said to take place 20 years earlier, in the late 1960s. The listener, a woman, claimed it was a true story that she experienced herself, and it took place not long after the Second World War. This is fitting with the hanten, which is a traditional short winter coat or vest that isn't commonly seen nowadays.

Inagawa reportedly investigated the woman's story himself and discovered that the school she was talking about was used by kamikaze pilots during the war. The pilots wrote their names on the toilet wall before they left to die for their country, and after the war was over, one of their mothers visited the school. She found the names scrawled on the wall, including her son's, and committed suicide. It was this mother's grudge that brought about the voice asking if anyone would like a red hanten.

Inagawa's telling of the tale involved the voice asking the question in a sing-song manner, a tune that he came up with himself. The tune became so popular that it still occasionally appears on television programs today, shocking Inagawa each time he hears it. You can find a full version of the song performed by Higuchi Mai on the CD *Junji Inagawa no Kaidan - Mystery Night Tour Selection 13 "Akai Hanten [Complete Edition]"*.

Of course, the story isn't true. It was likely influenced by the likes of Aka Manto and Hanako-san of the Toilet, but it is just another in the long list of *gakko kaidan*, school ghost stories.

SOCIETY

Mysterious Sticker

A young man arrived home one night and noticed something strange. There was a sticker on his doorplate, so small that he wouldn't have noticed it if he wasn't paying close attention. He had no memory of putting it there himself. Perhaps it was a joke by one of the kids in the neighbourhood, or even a salesman. The young man peeled the sticker off and, without thinking about it, placed it on the doorplate of the room opposite him.

A few days later, the young man arrived home to find the building in an uproar. There was even a police car downstairs. He reached his floor and found several police officers coming in and out of the apartment opposite his. He asked a neighbour he was friendly with what was going on. Apparently, the woman who lived in the apartment opposite his had a scuffle with thieves. She was stabbed, and they didn't know if she would pull through.

The police captured the thieves, who exclaimed, "Dammit! Nobody was supposed to be there during the day!"

ABOUT

Someone arrives home to find a sticker on their door they don't remember. Without giving it much thought, they peel it off and place it on the neighbour's door instead. A few days later, they discover said neighbour robbed and stabbed. The sticker was clearly a sign of reconnaissance by the thieves; a sign of an apartment that was supposed to be empty during the day and thus free for the taking.

According to a Japanese government survey taken in 2014, 70% of Tokyo residents lived in apartments. The average around the entire country was 42%. That's 9.36 million people in Tokyo, or 53.5 million people around Japan living in an apartment building that same year. With so many people living in apartments, urban legends about them are also on the rise.

There are tales of apartments without fourth floors, or no rooms with the number four (four, of course, being an unlucky number in Japan because it's also pronounced the same way as the word for "death"). Some legends even state that the number of stairs connecting the first floor to the second floor is always the same, and if you happen to come across a building that has a different number, that building is haunted.

This particular legend, however, seems to have begun life as an *imi ga wakaru to kowai hanashi*, a unique series of stories you can find on the internet that translates to "scary stories when you understand." Like creepypastas, these stories are written by anonymous authors and passed around until no-one knows where they originally came from anymore. At the end they come with an explanation, letting the reader know the hidden twist that makes the story scary in case they were unable to realise it for themselves. In this case, it's the realisation that the sticker was used as a sign by thieves of which houses to rob, and the young man unwittingly put his neighbour at risk by moving it to her door instead. But is there any truth to the story? Scarily, there is.

DOOR MARKING

This type of situation is called "door marking" and it's well known amongst salesmen, criminals, and the security firms that fight them. The original story that became an urban legend was likely inspired by this real practice. Often the marking is done in text, rather than a sticker (you can't peel text off), and a code has developed to let other people know about the occupants inside the house. For example:

- Several stickers indicate the number of times the house has been visited.
- Different colours indicate different months the house was visited.
- Black signifies a difficult house to deal with, whether that's a male occupant, a large family, never at home, etc.
- White signifies an easy target; usually a single woman, someone who always answers the door, someone who's likely to buy, etc.
- Yellow signifies someone who is on the fence, but could be sold something else.
- Gold signifies a house with money.

Other than stickers, kanji and English letters are also used:

- The kanji for student, meaning students live

inside.

- The Japanese letter "a" for *akachan*, or baby inside.
- The Japanese letter "i" for *ikeru*, meaning sales are possible here.
- The Japanese letter "ko" for *kowai*, meaning a scary household to deal with.

- The letter "M" for man inside.
- The letter "W" for woman inside.
- The letter "S" for a single person inside.
- The letters "SS" for someone who has weekends off inside.
- The letter "K" for *katta*, or someone who bought something.

- ◎ for a house with a contract completion.
- ○ for someone who will listen to salesmen before driving them off.
- X for a house that's no good; won't listen or often complains.
- ・ for a house that's been visited once before.
- 〆 for a house that's impossible to sell to.
- △ or ☆ for a house that's on the verge of buying, but hasn't tipped over the edge yet.

- "20" for a household occupant in their 20s.
- "1" for a household occupant that lives alone.
- "1017" for a household occupant that leaves at 10 a.m. and returns at 5 p.m.

There are, of course, other codes as well, and these codes are often combined. For example, a mark of "SW20 1017" on a letterbox would mean a single woman in her 20s who leaves the house at 10 and returns at 5. Kind of scary just how much information could be conveyed to other salesmen (and thieves) in just a few letters, huh?

The best way to avoid this is to regularly check your door and mailbox when coming home, and if you do find something that shouldn't be there, clean it off as soon as possible and alert the police. Defacing someone's house or building, even with stickers or text, is a criminal act under Article 1 Section 33 of the Minor Offences Act in Japan. Just make sure you don't move any stickers to a neighbour's house, because maybe they might end up like the woman in the legend….

Red Fundoshi

Sagawa Express. That company that roams the country's highways. Did you know that if you touch the picture of a postman wearing a red *fundoshi* on their trucks, it will bring you good fortune?

It's easy enough to touch the truck when it's parked, but if you're looking for even more luck, you need to touch the red fundoshi while the truck is moving.

ABOUT

Sagawa Express is one of the largest transportation companies in Japan. In the early 90s, their trucks were painted with the company's mascot, Hikyaku-kun, or Mr Postman, a courier designed like a sumo wrestler wearing a red fundoshi, or sumo underwear. Before long, rumours started to spread amongst elementary school students, and later high school students, that touching this mascot would bring happiness and wealth. Some even went so far as claiming that touching the backside of the drivers themselves would bring you good fortune (and not a sexual harassment lawsuit…). But how did such a rumour come about?

SAGAWA'S SCANDAL

Rumours that touching the red fundoshi of Sagawa's mascot started to spread in 1991. The rumours became so prevalent that Sagawa released a statement saying there was no truth to the matter.

In 1992, however, Sagawa's public image took a hit. It was revealed that Kanemaru Shin, a member of the ruling Liberal Democratic Party, received illegal donations to the tune of 500 million yen from Sagawa Express. The then-CEO of Sagawa, Watanabe Hiroyasu, was also revealed to have longtime connections to Ishii Susumi, a high-ranking member of the Inagawa-kai yakuza gang; a man he paid to help deal with troubles during the bubble economy of the 1980s. This scandal went all the way up to then-prime minister Hosokawa Morihiro (now-18th Head of the Kumamoto-Hosokawa clan, a clan who can trace their lineage back to the emperors of old). Hosokawa was forced to resign in April 1994 after it was revealed he had also received a loan from the company.

In order to combat the damage done to their public image, Sagawa took advantage of the urban legend proclaiming good fortune to all who touched their mascot and produced 300,000 "postman dolls to bring you happiness." They distributed these to customers as a form of public relations, and you can still buy these dolls on the internet today.

A short while later, the urban legend picked up steam amongst female high school students. Not only would you get good fortune, touching the red fundoshi would make you rich! After all, Kanemaru Shin received 500 million yen from the company and only had to pay back 200,000 of it before retiring! Easy money!

A CHANGE OF MASCOTS

Obviously, trying to touch a moving truck to receive good luck from its mascot was highly dangerous. Fearing the accidents that might occur from children trying to touch their trucks, Sagawa warned its drivers to always confirm the road was clear before taking off to avoid accidents. They then changed the design of the trucks themselves. In the late 90s, Hikyaku-kun was moved to the bottom corner of their delivery trucks while the body was painted in "galaxy colours," a mix of blue, white, and grey waves designed to look like a galaxy. Hikyaku-kun's red fundoshi was also removed from the design entirely, changed to red pants and a striped shirt.

In 2005 his design was retired, and in 2007 a new mascot was brought in. This one features a simplistic delivery man in blue pants and striped shirt holding a red parcel, no fundoshi in sight. No word on whether touching his red parcel brings good luck, but probably best not to try.

Car Guillotine

One day, an old woman decided to go for a drive with her grandchild. It was a brand new car, so she didn't yet understand the finer details of operating it. The child opened the window to enjoy the breeze, but that would prove to be a fatal mistake.

The child had a phone hanging from a strap around their neck. As they stuck their head out the window to take in the breeze, the strap caught on the window switch and, without realising, began to close it.

The old woman panicked, but was unable to figure out how to open the window again. Something crunched, and she soon realised it was the sound of her grandchild's neck breaking.

ABOUT

It's possible this legend is based on a real-life incident. In 2017, a two-year-old boy in South Carolina died after getting his neck caught in the window of his father's truck. The father stepped away briefly and when he came back, the boy was dead from asphyxiation. The windows were operated by a rocker-type switch, and it was believed the child accidentally stood on it while sticking his head out the window. But is an automatic window strong enough to break a human neck, like this legend claims?

Japanese TV performed various tests and discovered that most automatic windows were able to easily slice through something as thick as a daikon radish, and tests performed in the UK showed them slicing through an apple as well. However, there's no proof that they can actually break a human neck. The real danger, as with the child above, is death by asphyxiation.

It's smart not to stick your head out the window of a moving car regardless, but while a closing window might not break your neck, especially for children, the danger is very present and very real. Take care and always be aware of what's happening near automatic windows with children so you don't end up like the grandmother in this tale.

Yellow Ambulance

In this world, there are special cases that sit outside the norm. Even amongst ambulances you'll find such things. You might be used to the sight of pure white ambulances, but they say there is a special yellow type as well. This yellow ambulance is used to forcibly carry those who are mentally unstable to the hospital.

ABOUT

This legend also goes by the name "Yellow Pee-poh," with "pee-poh" being the sound that ambulance sirens make in Japanese. While yellow ambulances exist in other countries, ambulances in Japan are strictly white, as designated by the Road Traffic Law. The only exceptions to this rule are brown ambulances for the army and navy, and blue ambulances for the air-force. And yet, all over the country you can hear rumours of these supposed yellow ambulances that come not to carry injured or sick people to hospital, but to carry people away for mental illness.

Yellow is the most common colour, but depending on where you go, these ambulances can also be green, blue, or even purple in colour. The defining factor of these ambulances that aren't white is that they are designed to carry mentally unwell people away, and according to some versions, people can even get paid 3,000 to 5,000 yen for "tipping" the hospitals off to someone.

ORIGINS

Psychiatrist Kazano Haruki did research into this particular myth and discovered that it has existed since at least the 1970s. It appears to exist all over Japan, from the top of Tohoku all the way down to the bottom of Kyushu, with the main variance being the colour.

In 1973, a book written by Inoue Mitsuharu called *Animal Cemetery* featured a character who mentions that patients are taken to mental hospitals by yellow ambulances. This marks one of the first times the legend appeared in print, and no doubt played a part in helping spread the legend even further. A light novel written by Sakuraba Kazuki in 2004 called *Suitei Shojo* also featured a mental hospital with a yellow ambulance.

One potential origin for the yellow ambulance myth has been traced to the movie *Yabai Koto Nara Zeni ni Naru*, released in 1962. One scene features a yellow propaganda car proclaiming that patients have escaped from a Tokyo mental institution. Kazano has argued that claiming this movie to be the origin of the myth is a bit of a stretch, but others still believe it to be the case.

The American movie *One Flew Over the Cuckoo's Nest*, released in Japan in 1976, featured patients being transferred from a mental hospital in a yellow vehicle. With how often the colour yellow has appeared in media associated with mental hospitals, people have argued that this movie also helped strengthen the myth as it first came to life.

Others have suggested that highway patrol cars

may not be the cause of the myth, but at the very least solidified it. Patrol cars throughout Japan are generally yellow, although they can vary from prefecture to prefecture, and feature flashing lights on top just like an ambulance. It's possible that young children mistook them for ambulances and came to believe that the stories were true, spreading the legend through word of mouth and believing that they had seen the infamous yellow ambulances for real.

Another argument suggests that the association comes from the word "yellow" itself. In Japanese, yellow is pronounced *ki*. There are several slang words, such as *kijirushi* or *kichigai*, that are used to describe a "madman" or "lunatic." This use of *ki* in both words gives them an association with yellow, and thus, yellow ambulances designed to take "madmen" away.

While the exact origins are unknown, the association of yellow with mental illness has come up multiple times over the years, ensuring that this legend continues to be spread until this day.

Kokkai-gijidomae Station

There is a subway station in Nagata-chou, Chiyoda Ward, Tokyo, which is called Kokkai-gijidomae Station. Just like its name states, it's located near the National Diet Building, and it has a special function. In an emergency, it's said that this station can also act as a nuclear shelter. Members of parliament and other bureaucrats can quickly escape, and in a worst-case scenario that sees Tokyo wiped out, they will be able to survive.

ABOUT

There are numerous legends about the subways and tunnels beneath Tokyo, and this one claims that Kokkai-gijidomae Station is not just a mere subway station, but a nuclear bomb shelter as well. The station is run by Tokyo Metro and runs on the Chiyoda and Marunouchi Lines. It opened on March 15, 1959, and as of 2017, saw roughly 150,000 people pass through its ticket gates each day. It also holds the record for being the deepest underground station in the entire Tokyo Metro network; it's located 37.9 metres underneath the surface. It's important to note that Kokkai-gijidomae Station isn't the deepest station in Tokyo, however. That honour belongs to Roppongi Station, which is located 42 metres underground. So how and when did rumours first start circulating that Kokkai-gijidomae was doubling as a secret nuclear bomb shelter?

HISTORY

During the Second World War, the Imperial army began digging beneath the surface of Tokyo to construct air raid shelters. The war was over before most of this construction was finished, and the public were never informed of just where and how far construction had gone before it was halted. That alone is enough for urban legends to spring to life, but there's more to the story.

In 1960, Prime Minister Kishi Nobusuke was pursuing a new security treaty with the United States. Many of the public, however, were in opposition with these reforms. Over 100,000 students surrounded the National Diet Building with the idea that "If the prime minister can't get inside, then he can't sign the new deal." The joke was on them, however, as Prime Minister Kishi calmly appeared inside the building and signed the new treaty. How did he get in?

He certainly didn't enter through the outside; it was impossible for anyone to get through the massive crowd. It didn't take long to hit upon the only potential answer; he reached the building via the underground. He had to have entered through a secret underground tunnel; a tunnel linking the National Diet Building with the prime minister's official residence.

The prime minister's official residence is located directly above Kokkai-gijidomae Station. The station officially opened only a year before the protests in 1960, but construction had been ongoing for much longer. At present there *is* an underground tunnel that connects the prime minister's official residence, the House of Representatives, and the National Diet. However, this tunnel wasn't completed until 1963, three years after the prime minister mysteriously appeared inside the National Diet Building. To this day, no information has ever been given as to how the prime minister managed to get inside, but the most likely explanation lies underground.

The tunnel connecting the official government buildings in Chiyoda Ward has gradually been enlarged and expanded upon over the years, but the original bomb shelter beneath the prime minister's official residence was completed in 1942. It featured a tunnel allowing those inside to escape in case of an emergency, but there were plans for another tunnel connecting it to the National Diet Building at the time as well. This tunnel was designed to be built roughly 13 to 14 metres underground, but the war was over before construction was completed. Nobody knows how far construction got before the project was called off, but considering the prime minister was secretly able to access the National Diet Building without travelling above ground, it doesn't seem much of a stretch to assume the tunnel was completed to a degree that at least allowed people to pass through.

MODERN TIMES

So how does all of this connect to Kokkai-gijidomae Station acting as a bomb shelter? Urban legends, by their nature, change and grow over time, adding embellishments and taking whatever information is necessary to make them seem more believable. An air raid shelter was built beneath the prime minister's official residence during the Second World War. This much is known. A tunnel was planned to connect that air raid shelter to the National Diet Building. This much is also known. There's a good chance it was already completed, or construction continued even after the war ended, but regardless, an official tunnel connecting the buildings was completed in the early 1960s, several years after rumours that there was a secret tunnel anyway.

Kokkai-gijidomae Station is one of the deepest subway stations in all of Tokyo, was completed in the late 50s, and it sits right under the prime minister's official residence. It's not terribly difficult to connect all the dots and see why people might start talking about the station itself featuring a hidden bomb shelter.

THE TRUTH?

An internet writer by the handle of "Yoppy" did an interview with a Tokyo Metro employee in December 2017. Amongst various other urban legends said to exist in the Tokyo subways, he asked whether there was any truth to the rumours that Kokkai-gijidomae Station featured a secret tunnel leading to a bomb shelter that only VIPs could access. The answer, of course, was "no." The employee claimed that Tokyo Metro had nothing to do with the government or the self-defence forces, and the rumours likely started because of how deep the station is located underground. The reason the station is located so far down is because of the topography of the area around the Chiyoda Line, and because it must also go underneath the Hibiya Line which runs above it.

It was his belief that rumours like these started because people were able to see trains and platforms on other lines that weren't for regular use. If they weren't for regular use, then of course they must be for secret use, when the reality is much more mundane. These platforms and lines exist for maintenance and forwarding. Nothing more. Any secret passages, doors, and platforms were simply for maintenance workers to do their jobs underground, and to house the electricity that powers the station.

Beneath the Research University

Beneath a certain research university you'll find a road. This road leads to an underground research facility in which they perform terrifying experiments around the clock. If you continue even further down the path, it takes you to three separate train stations.

ABOUT

It's thought this legend is talking about the University of Tsukuba in Ibaraki Prefecture, due to the specific mention of the nearby stations, but it could technically be anywhere, which is the point. This legend came to be because several universities now exist on ground that were used by the Imperial army during the war, so of course, there must be secret research facilities still hidden on the grounds where nefarious wartime research continues. Because they have electricity lines that run underground, they must be powering these facilities even to this day.

Needless to say, the likelihood that any modern universities in Japan are carrying on nefarious research in underground labs built by the Imperial army is low to nil..

Skylark Billboard

Skylark, the popular family restaurant, features a caricature of a skylark on its billboards, but did you know that there's actually a male version and a female version?

It's incredibly easy to tell them apart. The skylark with a bellybutton drawn on its stomach is the male, while the skylark with no bellybutton is the female. Some of the female skylarks are also caring for eggs, and if you mention this to the staff you will get as much free coffee as you want.

The rarest of all is the female skylark billboard with some of her eggs hatching. If you happen to see and mention this one to the staff, you'll receive a free slice of cake as well.

ABOUT

Skylark was a popular family restaurant chain in Japan. The first store opened on July 7, 1970, and was supposedly named because the hill near where it operated was home to numerous skylarks. The chain experienced massive growth over the years, but in October 2009, it was announced that all remaining Skylark restaurants would be rebranding to Gusto, another chain owned by the same company.

It's unknown when this rumour about the male and female skylarks first started, but it's likely that it sprang to life in 1975, not too long after Skylark billboards around the country were updated with a (slightly) newer logo design. The original Skylark logo is what people now call the female. This design had no bellybutton, just like the legend states. However, in 1975, two small lines were added to the bird's stomach, giving it the appearance of a bellybutton. Not all billboards across the country were updated with this new design, which meant some birds had bellybuttons and some didn't. It's not too hard to see why people might take this to mean that some birds were male, and some birds were female. If that were the case, what was the meaning behind it?

THE TRUTH

Of course, there was no meaning. It's expensive to update billboards, especially over something so small, and thus many stores continued to run the old ones. Then, why even add a bellybutton to a bird in the first place? According to management at the time, customers adored the Skylark logo, and the company wished for their restaurants to be seen as the heart of the communities they resided in. For this reason, the logo was given a bellybutton, a visible sign of the connection between mother and child; a visible sign of "family."

So, if there was no male or female Skylark, was it possible to receive free coffee if you pointed this out? Sadly, no. This too was just a rumour, and if you happened to notice a different billboard outside a restaurant and pointed this out to the staff, you wouldn't get anything free. What about the eggs? If you spotted the rarest of all billboards, the Skylark looking after her eggs, could you at least get some free cake?

According to the Skylark public relations department at the time, “We’ve heard rumours about the male and female characters, but this is the first time we’ve heard about eggs.” The eggs themselves were just a rumour, and nobody has ever given proof that such a billboard existed.

This urban legend appears to have come about thanks to a simple design change, growing to take on a life of its own and even creating a mythical billboard that never existed in the first place. No free coffee or cakes were ever given out for pointing out billboard differences, and now, all the billboards are gone for good. Skylark, the happy little bird with a bellybutton, is now but a memory and a legend that continues to live on long after all its stores closed down.

Cell Phone Abuse

We've all had a cell phone we've finished using. Do you by any chance take those phones to a trader or phone shop? If so, you might be in for a dangerous surprise…

The reason for that is because there are small phone stores and traders who collect old phones in order to extract the information left within them. Your personal details, the people you know, the people you've called; there are companies that collect it all.

If you do happen to leave your old phone with one of these companies, chances are they've already leaked your associations, as well as any work secrets you may have left on your phone.

ABOUT

According to statistics, 107.1 million people in Japan owned a cell phone in 2018. Considering the population is roughly 126.8 million, that's a lot of people with cell phones, and a lot of people getting rid of their old ones to upgrade to the newest and fanciest models. But what happens to those old phones once you take them to the store to trade in or dispose of?

It might seem common sense to clear all of your information from a phone before you hand it over for good, but this urban legend is yet another reminder that there are people out there who would happily take your personal information and use it for their own gain. This legend seems to target small shops and traders in particular, with the reasoning being small shops struggle to compete with large companies and they can only stay afloat by illegally selling information. It's not a terribly large leap to wonder why a small corner store can sell its phones so cheap and offer great rates on trade ins if they're making their real money from selling your personal info.

Is there any truth to the matter? It is, of course, impossible to make sweeping generalisations such as "all stores sell personal information" or "no stores sell personal information." There's a good chance that someone, somewhere, is extracting whatever information they can from old phones that have been traded in and using it for their own financial gain.

It's both good practice and common sense to delete any personal information from a phone before you hand it over to someone else for good, even if that someone is a professional business. This urban legend is yet another reminder of that, and a stern warning of what might happen if you don't.

Interview Photos

Job hunting season has a huge influence over the direction one's life takes, but there is one legend that numerous big city dwellers believe in. That is, if you take a photo for your interview card at the department store Isetan, you will be guaranteed the job of your dreams.

Announcers such as Kisa Ayako and Uozumi Rie were also blessed with their dream jobs after having their photos taken at the studio inside Isetan. So many people believe in this legend that every year when job hunting season rolls around, the photo studio becomes incredibly busy.

ABOUT

Job hunting season for new graduates in Japan usually begins around October, with the aim of a full-time job when the new business year starts in April. Part of this process involves an interview card, which is basically a survey of who you are, your work and education history, why you want the job, and where specifically you'd like to work. Basically a resume, but in a more rigid format. This interview card is accompanied by a head shot—hopefully professionally taken—so interviewers know who they're dealing with. There are a lot of superstitions when it comes to job hunting season, but this is one of the more widely known ones.

Isetan Photo Studio can be found in Shinjuku, and they come highly recommended for a reason: they take damn good photos. So good that people are willing to spend up to ten times the amount of having a photo taken in a regular passport booth. They also do slight editing upon request, meaning they can smooth out wrinkles, fix tiny flaws, and make you look better than ever. The morals of editing a photo meant to help secure you a job aside, Isetan Photo Studio gets results, and that keeps people coming back.

Isetan sees over 10,000 customers a year. During job hunting season, they often deal with over 300 customers in a single day. Their powers aren't just limited to new recruits, however. Those who are changing jobs and need to spruce up their resume with a new head shot also praise their results, and some have even visited them to get head shots taken for junior and high school entrance exams.

One father posted on his blog about how his wife made their son take photos at Isetan Photo Studio for his junior high exam applications. His son was accepted to every school he applied to… except for one. The only school they didn't use an Isetan photo for. Coincidence? Possibly, but there is no denying that first impressions are very important in Japan, and when it comes to something like an application, a professionally taken photo stands out amongst the masses.

Is Isetan Photo Studio doing divine work and securing all of their job seekers the careers of their dreams? Of course not. But, thanks to their highly professional photos they *do* have an incredible track record, and when your future is on the line, what's a few extra thousand yen for something that stands out amongst the crowd? That's how legends like this continue to thrive, after all…

Arm Wrestling Machine

You can find arm wrestling machines in large arcades all across the country. If you visit with a large group of people and try to beat the computer, everyone can have a great time.

However, the strength of old arm wrestling machines used to be set too high, and numerous people broke their arms while challenging the computer. Adjusting the power of the machines was difficult, and people who went to arcades with their partners or friends didn't want to appear weak in front of them, causing them to go too far.

Of course, all these old machines were rounded up and the difficulty settings changed. Now, people complain that they are too weak, causing their owners even more troubles.

ABOUT

Arcades, or game centres, are still a massive business in Japan. My tiny little town in the middle of nowhere had a game centre that took up a large part of the shopping centre's top floor, and it was by far not the only one in town (and was, perhaps ironically, one of the smallest). In bigger cities you can find game centres that take up almost entire buildings, their games split by levels; UFO catchers and physical games like *Dance Dance Revolution* or *Taiko no Tatsujin* on the bottom floor to draw people in, and then other games like fighting, retro, simulators, etc on higher levels.

Arcades show no sign of slowing down in Japan.

According to a survey by *Jamma*, arcades in Japan made 433.8 billion yen in 2016 from 14,862 stores nationwide. They're big business, and things like arm wrestling machines are front door material. They draw customers in; they create crowds; they get people excited and spending money. But do they also break arms?

In this case, the answer is yes. You may have seen footage of people breaking their arms while arm wrestling a real opponent, but if you were wondering whether a machine could do the same, ask three men who challenged the machines over a two-week period in August 2007. The men, one from France, one from Korea, and the other Japanese, attempted to beat arm wrestling machines in Osaka, Kyoto, and Fukuoka, but all ended up breaking their arms instead.

According to Atlus, the company that owned the machines, they were previously owned by another company where they had numerous faults and problems. When Atlus bought them, they changed the name of the games and lowered the strength setting to disassociate them from their previous dangerous image. The company recalled all their machines after the incidents to investigate the cause of the problem once more, but the damage was done. News quickly spread of people breaking bones while using these machines in arcades and as a result, very few arm wrestling machines made it back to the field. Like other games that involve punching, kicking, or testing your strength, these days the arm wrestling machines are near impossible to find.

Meaning Behind the Kanji for "Road"

The kanji for "road" is used in many words: street, oesophagus, tool, etc. People write it every day without thinking about the meaning behind its make up.

On the left, you have the radical for "advance," meaning to proceed or go forward. Next to that you have the kanji for "head." It turns out there is an old, terrifying reason for why these two elements are used together to mean "road."

In Ancient China, it was common for people to cut off the heads of outsiders and proceed down a path with the head in their hands. This head would cleanse the path and protect the bearer from evil, and that is how the kanji for "road" came to be.

ABOUT

Chinese characters, or kanji as they're called in Japan, are often made up of various elements that signify the character's meaning at first glance. For example, the characters for "sun" and "moon" placed together makes a character meaning "bright."

Chinese characters have been around for 1000s of years, and it's believed they made their way to Japanese shores on Chinese gold seals in 57 AD. It wasn't until much later that Chinese literacy would increase amongst Japanese nobles, who had no written alphabet of their own, and it wasn't until the Heian Period (794-1185) that Japanese speakers began to arrange Chinese characters in a way that fit the Japanese language structure. They then derived their own writing style from these characters called manyogana, which later evolved into what we now know as hiragana and katakana.

These kanji all have a meaning, and that meaning is often represented in how the different parts of the character are put together. The kanji for "road" uses the radical "to proceed" alongside the character for "head." Most modern kanji users don't think deeply about the meaning of the character when they see it, however. It means "road." That's it. But if you stop to look at it and really think about what it means, suddenly it becomes a lot scarier. Proceeding with a head creates a road? How is that possible? What does it even mean?

THE TRUTH

As it turns out, this legend is true. In Ancient China, it was believed that carrying the head of your foe would cleanse an area of evil. Therefore, proceeding with a head in hand meant one was going down a path, or walking down a road. According to some legends, these heads would actually be buried by the side of the road leading into one's territory because it was thought this would stop the enemy from coming in to attack. According to others, the heads were carried like lanterns to dispel evil from a path. Makes that lantern yokai Chouchin Obake just a little more terrifying, doesn't it?

Either way, heads proceeding down a path came

to mean "road," and it's not the only kanji with a horrifying origin story. For example, the kanji for "take" is made up of two elements: on the left, an ear, and on the right, a hand. In Ancient China, cutting off the ears of one's enemies was a way of counting how many were defeated in battle. A hand taking an ear. Take. Perhaps the meaning behind this character was easier to imagine when ear cutting was a more common practice than it is today…

Many modern kanji have little resemblance to their original meanings or how they came to be. Depending on your point of view, perhaps it's sometimes better not to know.

Lake Shikotsu

In the past, Lake Shikotsu was spelt using the kanji for "death" and "bones." The reason for this was because if somebody died in the lake, their body would get tangled in the trees and weeds at the bottom and never again rise to the surface. The lake has a strong association with death, and that's why they call it Shikotsu.

ABOUT

Lake Shikotsu is a large lake in Chitose City, Hokkaido, just south of Sapporo City. With a circumference of roughly 40 kilometres, an average depth of 265 metres, and a maximum depth of 363 metres, Shikotsu is the second deepest lake in Japan, and measures about three quarters the volume of Lake Biwa, the largest lake in Japan.

The native people of Hokkaido, the Ainu, called the lake "shikot." When the Japanese arrived in Hokkaido, it sounded to them a lot like "shikotsu." *Shi* meaning death and *kotsu* meaning bones. No doubt the initial Japanese were terrified of this giant death lake full of bones, but to the Ainu "shikot" only meant a deep hollow.

In 1805, the Shikotsu River, which flows out of Lake Shikotsu, was renamed to Chitose River. To the Japanese who had moved in to claim the land, the name "shikotsu" sounded too much like a bad omen, so it was changed to the much nicer Chitose, meaning "a crane lives for a thousand years, a turtle for ten thousand." The area was full of cranes, so it seemed fitting and less grim. Later, the area itself was also renamed to Chitose, but for some unknown reason, the lake remains known as Shikotsu, even today.

But no, Lake Shikotsu is not full of the bones of the dead. This legend came about thanks to a simple linguistic misunderstanding.

Earthquakes and Akihabara

If a large-scale earthquake were ever to strike Tokyo, it's said that Akihabara would be the worst place to be.

These days, idol events take place in Akihabara on an almost daily basis. The idols sing and dance while their passionate fans (called "otaku") join them in a dance they call *otagei*. The fans jump up and dance in rhythm to the beat, creating quite the racket.

For that reason, it's said that the buildings around Akihabara are slowly losing their earthquake resistance thanks to the constant jumping and beating from idol fans. If a large earthquake were to strike Tokyo, the abused buildings of Akihabara would not be able to withstand it.

ABOUT

Idol fans in Japan are known for a particular dance they do called *otagei* or *wotagei* (the "w" is silent). This involves a lot of jumping high on the spot, furious arm thrusting, twirling, clapping, and chanting. Akihabara, being the idol hub of Japan in modern times, is the area you're most likely to see this type of dance being performed. The first time I saw it for myself was in Shibuya, not Akihabara, but thanks to the dominance of AKB48 and the idol culture that has built up in Akihabara in recent years, these days it's mostly associated with that area. A little searching on the internet will drop you into a strange rabbit hole if you are unaware of what the spectacle looks like. Watch a video or two and you'll soon get the idea.

Needless to say, buildings in Japan, and especially in Tokyo, are specially designed to withstand earthquakes. Roughly 1,500 earthquakes strike Japan each year, and often those earthquakes can be devastating. All buildings in Japan are required to be earthquake-resistant and must meet strict standards as set by the law. As of 2018, the Tokyo Metropolis area had a population of more than 13 million, while the Tokyo Metro area had a population of more than 38 million. That's a lot of potential deaths for a city constantly shaken by earthquakes.

Japan is constantly at the forefront of new technologies to prevent disasters like those in the past ever occurring again, and the government has spent billions of dollars to put systems in place to protect its people. A few guys jumping up and down every day in rhythm with their favourite idols? Yeah, it doesn't take a genius to realise that that's not going to weaken the structural integrity of some of the most powerful buildings in the world literally designed to withstand constant shaking.

As an interesting side note, Chiyoda City, where Akihabara can be found, is actually considered one of the safest regions in all of Tokyo. The Chiyoda, Minato, and Shibuya wards are where most foreign companies have their offices, and are therefore more modern and high-tech than the outlying areas of Tokyo. If a large earthquake were to strike, the areas along the Arakawa River and Sumidagawa River in the west are considered to be at the most risk, due to their old wooden buildings and densely gathered light-steel structures.

MEDICAL

Human-faced Carbuncle

A young man went to Tokyo University's culture festival one year. He was looking at the medical facility's exhibit and chatting to the professor when the professor asked him if he would like to see their medical forensics room.

The man was greatly interested and followed the professor. "If you're unsure, this is your last chance to leave," the professor said and then went into the room. The man followed him in. He saw numerous dead bodies floating in formalin, all lined up. Several of them were deformed, and there were jars of all sizes.

"Let me show you something special," the professor said and directed the man to a single glass jar. Inside was a clump of brown flesh about the size of a fist.

It was a human-faced carbuncle.

Apparently, it had been removed from a woman's knee in the middle of the Meiji Era, so not even the university had a record of the full details behind it.

ABOUT

The human-faced carbuncle, known in Japanese as *jinmensou*, is actually a yokai that's been around since at least the 1600s. Monk and author Asai Ryoui wrote about one in the ninth volume of his *Otogi Bouko*. The story goes that a peasant who lived in what is now modern day Ujishi City, Kyoto Prefecture, started to gradually become sicker and sicker. Six months passed when his left leg started to swell. Aside from being extremely painful, the swelling also happened to resemble a human face with eyes and a mouth.

Somewhat intrigued, the peasant tried putting sake in the swelling's mouth. It turned red, like it was drunk. He tried feeding it food, and the swelling ate it. He discovered that when he fed it, his pain receded, but when he stopped, the pain came roaring back. The peasant was soon nothing but skin and bones. He visited various doctors, but none could help him. He prepared himself for the worst.

It was then that a pilgrim came to see him. He revealed that he knew how to heal the swelling, so the peasant sold all his fields to pay the man. The pilgrim used the money to gather various ingredients, then one by one put them in the swelling's mouth. The mouth swallowed them all except for the fritillaria verticillata flower, which it refused. The pilgrim then ground the flower into a fine powder and forced it into the mouth. 17 days later, it was completely gone.

Sightings of these human-faced swellings continued over the years, although recent improvements in science and medicine have some claiming that the origins of this yokai stem from elephantiasis. There are numerous wooden carvings and illustrations of the human-faced carbuncle from history, but how did one end up in Tokyo University?

The story is, of course, just a story. Is there a chance that Tokyo University has something that resembles a human face cut from another human's body? Possibly. The university is one of the largest in Japan with a long history, which is how these stories come to life in the first place. Where there's medical research, there are rumours, and that's why stories like this one continue to thrive.

Diet Capsule

"With one single pill, you too can easily lose weight!"

There was an ad in a fashion magazine proclaiming that with a single, suspicious pill you could easily lose weight. Of course, most people would smell it for the shit it was and skip over it, but for one troubled young woman, who had tried anything and everything to lose weight, she was drawn in.

'Although, I doubt this one will do anything either…' she thought.

A few days later, her capsule arrived.

"This capsule is extremely effective, so only take one. However, please refrain from alcohol or spicy foods, as they may react badly with it."

The woman was suspicious, but she swallowed the capsule anyway. Its effects were even better than she imagined! The weight melted off her, even without exercise, and she could eat as much as she wanted. She went from the shape of a round pear to that of a model.

It wasn't all smooth sailing, however. Shortly after swallowing the pill, the woman was troubled by stomach pains. The thinner she got, the worse the pain grew. Finally she couldn't stand it anymore and went to see the doctor.

After examining her, the doctor was shocked. It turned out there was a tapeworm, several meters long, living in her intestines. Inside that capsule had been a tapeworm egg.

ABOUT

It's not known when this legend spread to Japan specifically, but the tapeworm diet itself has been around since at least the Victorian Era. In their efforts to fit the Victorian ideal of beauty, women underwent many horrific procedures and diets to achieve their desired look. One of these was the tapeworm diet, which is exactly what it sounds like: swallowing a tapeworm and letting it live inside you so it consumes what you eat and you don't put on weight. Sadly, the tapeworm diet didn't die with the Victorian Era, but continues to live on to this day.

These days, like the urban legend above, you can buy pills that have a tapeworm egg inside. You swallow the pill, the egg hatches in your intestines, and then you're on your way to weight loss city. In 2013, a woman in Iowa visited her doctor and admitted she bought a tapeworm pill off the internet, and she's hardly alone. Khloe Kardashian suggested she wanted to get a tapeworm to lose weight on *Keeping Up with the Kardashians*. Tyra Banks spoke to women on her talk show in 2009 who said they would be willing to swallow tapeworms if it meant losing weight, and in 2010, Hong Kong's Department of Health warned people against buying parasite eggs online to lose weight. Popular Italian singer Maria Callas is perhaps one of the most famous people accused of using the tapeworm diet to lose weight, although she denied ever swallowing one willingly for that purpose (she instead was unknowingly infected with one while eating).

A tapeworm inside your intestines will help you lose weight, of course. But there's also a good chance it will kill you, not to mention the diarrhoea, abdomen pain, nausea, fever, fatigue, bacterial infections, and neurological issues that come along with it. You would think it would be common sense not to buy a mystery diet pill claiming to solve all your weight problems without any effort, but as they say, common sense isn't very common anymore. Never buy a random pill off the internet and swallow it, no matter how badly you might want to lose weight.

Game Brain

Do you like video games? Of course, video games are fun, but if you play them constantly, it's dangerous for your health. If you play games every day for a long period of time, I want you to listen carefully to what I have to say, because it's likely that you already have "game brain."

Games use simple, repetitive actions, and those lower the capacity of your brain's frontal regions. This leaves you in a state not too dissimilar to dementia. Playing games for too long will leave you unable to control yourself, making you quick to anger and more likely to commit crimes. The only way to avoid game brain is to stop playing games immediately and live a healthy life.

ABOUT

If you made it this far without laughing, you're a better person than I am. This urban legend sprang to life thanks to a professor from Nihon University named Mori Akio. In 2002, he published a book called *The Terror of Game Brain*. He performed an experiment looking at the effect of playing video games on the human brain and determined that playing for a long period of time had a negative effect on brain waves. This lack of activity in the brain's prefrontal region meant that video gamers had less control over their emotions and creativity than people who didn't play games. As a result, they experienced more fatigue and inability to concentrate, were quicker to anger, and had problems socialising with others.

You've no doubt seen this argument provided yourself in your own country. Video games are evil and they're making our children criminals. There is, of course, no evidence that this is true, and it wasn't long until scientists challenged Mori's beliefs, as well as the experiment itself. Some brain specialists argued that Mori used unreliable measures and misinterpreted the data. Others suggested that fatigue was the real cause, not gaming.

THE EVIDENCE AGAINST

Kawashima Ryuta, a Japanese neuroscientist, released a book in 2003 called *Train Your Brain: 60 Days to a Better Brain*. He later turned this book into a video game called *Brain Age: Train your Brain in Minutes a Day!*. He argued that Mori's idea of "game brain" was merely a superstition, and he continues his work on video games to this day.

In 2005, Baba Akira, a professor from the University of Tokyo, held an interview with *ITMedia*. He mentioned that the term "game brain" was only used in Japan and that, if you mentioned the term to someone overseas, they would laugh at you. He argued that because the media took Mori's claims at face value without doing any research or critical thinking themselves, they caused an entire generation of parents to worry over nothing.

Baba argued that there were two major problems with Mori's experiment. First, his method of measuring brain waves. Mori performed his test on university students and elementary school students who were out enjoying a campus festival. He used a simple machine to measure their brain waves, but brain waves aren't something that can be so easily measured. You can't just stick a hat on someone like in a manga and accurately measure their brain.

Secondly, Mori's claims that the alpha and beta waves of the prefrontal cortex of the brain simplified while playing games, resembling that of dementia patients, was a poor explanation. Baba argued that as people get used to playing games, the activity in the prefrontal cortex naturally cools down. Another part of the brain takes over because it's no longer a new action, so this isn't evidence that games are turning brains to mush, but evidence that the gamers were growing accustomed to the movements of the game.

Habu Yoshiharu, a professional shogi player, had his brain waves recorded and showed very little activity in his prefrontal cortex while playing. By Mori's logic, Habu, an extremely intelligent man, also suffered from game brain and wasn't just well accustomed to the game he made his profession. In fact, the same could be said for anyone who was skilled at something, not just games.

Several Japanese professors and neuroscientists, such as Tsumoto Tadaharu, have come out over the years to dismiss the idea of "game brain," and most now regard it as pseudoscience. However, the splash it made in the media when it was first revealed was so strong that the idea still persists in Japan today. It makes sense to not allow children to play video games for 10 hours straight, but it's not because of the dementia and criminal behaviour it will cause in them. Even so, it might be awhile before this urban legend is finally buried for good.

Lowering of Scalpels

Countrywide, June is often known as the "lowering of scalpels." It's called this because it's when new surgeons begin performing operations for the first time. Every April, brand new doctors begin working in hospitals, and after two months of training, June marks the first time they pick up their scalpels and begin operating for real. In general, they are given easy operations such as removing appendixes to begin with, and for that reason, June is known as the "lowering of scalpels."

ABOUT

In contrast to other parts of the world, the Japanese school and business years begin in April. Fresh workers will generally spend the first few months of the working year undergoing training and acclimatising to their new work environment. While this legend references doctors and the mass number of surgeons performing for the first time around June, it's applicable to any profession. Most new workers won't really start doing their jobs until around June, and *mesu oroshi*, or lowering of scalpels, can be used more figuratively for all new workers diving in for the first time.

Sleep-talking

Every now and then people talk in their sleep. However, you mustn't talk back to them. If you do, they will die.

ABOUT

This is a fairly popular "common sense" urban legend in Japan. You mustn't talk to somebody who is sleep-talking, otherwise they will die. Of course, if somebody is talking to you in their sleep, you may be tempted to talk back. It's rude not to answer, and if somebody appears to be afraid or concerned, even in their sleep, it's human nature to want to help. But, according to this legend, you shouldn't. Why? Well, there are various reasons. Let's take a look at some.

NO TALKING

The first reason is the belief that when somebody is talking in their sleep, it's because they're talking to a ghost. It makes sense that you wouldn't want to interrupt that and bring the wrath of the spirit down upon you. However, it's believed that if you interrupt a spirit having a conversation with a sleeping person, the spirit won't take their anger out on you, but the person sleeping instead. They will take that person's spirit with them when they leave, presumably to finish the conversation elsewhere, and so the person will die.

Even if the spirit doesn't steal their soul away,

interrupting their conversation may still shorten that person's lifespan, cause them mental damage, or cause them to simply never wake up again and spend the rest of their natural life in a coma.

A spirit stealing a soul away because their conversation with a sleeping person was interrupted is hardly very scientific, however. While this particular belief has been around for a while, a slightly more scientific explanation claims you shouldn't speak back because you'll be interrupting their REM sleep, and this isn't a good thing either.

When we sleep, we pass in and out of REM and non-REM sleep. Non-REM sleep is the deep phase where both the brain and body are at rest. REM sleep, on the other hand, is more shallow. The brain is actively working while the body is at rest. It's during this time that people may sleep-talk, and if you reply to them, you are essentially messing with their sleep, which will leave the person feeling even more exhausted when they wake up. Or, so the belief goes.

Long before scientific studies into sleep and what goes on in the brain were conducted, people had no idea what was happening when someone started to talk. It made sense that they were probably talking to a ghost. Then, as science progressed, maybe they weren't talking to ghosts, but it still wasn't good to reply because you would mess with their sleep schedule instead.

At any rate, it's probably best not to converse with people when they are sleep-talking; first, they're unlikely to make much sense, and second, that's your precious sleep time as well. If their sleep-talking is that bad, then it might be time for a visit to the doctor, but simply replying to them won't cause them to die like this legend would have you believe. Like many urban legends, it was born long ago due to lack of understanding and spread enough that, even today, it (ironically) refuses to die.

Cup Noodles and Blood Donations

Cup noodles are wildly popular the world over. In Japan especially, young people eat them on a near-daily basis. But amongst these people, there is something strange taking place, and it's taking place in their blood.

A young man went to donate blood one day. However, before the nurse could take any, she said, "I'm afraid you can't donate today."

The young man had never had any problems before, so he asked her why. The nurse was reluctant, but finally she answered.

"We found oil floating in your blood. By any chance, do you happen to eat cup noodles every day?"

ABOUT

This legend started to spread on the internet just recently. There are plenty of reasons not to eat instant ramen every day; high amounts of sodium, few nutrients, MSG, etc, but discovering oil in your blood from eating too much isn't one of them. You can still donate your blood, and who knows, if you're in an area that pays for donations, maybe you can afford a meal better than cup noodles afterwards as well!

If you believe the rumours, oil in your blood isn't the only problem eating too many cup noodles causes. Another common legend goes as follows:

While sales of cup noodles are on the rise the

world over, something opposite is happening within our bodies. That is, men's sperm counts are decreasing.

This isn't exclusive to cup noodles, but many fast foods contain chemical seasonings. They are weakening people's reproductive processes. As a result, it's becoming difficult to ignore the effect it's having on men's sperm counts.

Various studies have been done over the years connecting dropping sperm counts and nutrition. One study performed by Baylor University and Harvard discovered that eating instant noodles two or more times a week was linked to several health issues, including the potential for miscarriages and lowered sperm production. Once again, it makes sense not to base your diet around instant noodles, but in this case, there may be at least a little truth behind the legend.

Helmet

A group of friends were on a bike trip when one of the men slipped and fell, colliding head-first with a guardrail. He hit the rail with incredible speed, and his friends panicked, rushing over to him.

"I'm okay, I'm okay!" The man abruptly jumped up and waved at his friends.

The men were relieved. He didn't appear to have any injuries, either.

"Take it easy. You didn't hurt yourself, did you?" They laughed with the man and teased him.

"My bad, I accidentally turned the handle the wrong way and screwed up. But yeah, my head kinda does hurt a little."

The man removed his helmet and his friends screamed. His head was caved in, and as soon as the helmet was off, the man collapsed. It turned out that when the man crashed into the guardrail, his head had turned to mush inside his helmet and that helmet was the only thing keeping it all together.

ABOUT

Common first aid tells us not to remove a person's helmet if they've been in an accident. If you remove an injured person's helmet, you may exacerbate their injuries, and it should generally only be done if there is a clear and present choking danger. In this legend, however, the helmet itself is what's keeping the man's head together, and once that pressure is gone, he dies instantly.

Full-face helmets found general use in Japan

from the early 1960s, and by the late 80s these full-face helmets came with movable shield protectors as well. They're now the norm for bike riders (although you still get the occasional riders who enjoy the half-style or old fashioned helmets), but it's likely the rise in popularity of these full-face helmets, said to give you the best protection, gave birth to this legend.

That being said, this legend is obviously just a story. The helmet itself would crack before the man's skull inside it turned to mush, and here the helmet is still intact and the only thing keeping the man's brain and skull together. It's a cautionary tale meant to scare, but if you hit a guardrail hard enough to turn your skull to pieces, I'd worry more about your spine and other vital organs also giving out then whether a helmet is the only thing keeping your head together.

Kendo and Baldness

High level kendo practitioners spend long periods of time practising with their masks on, which then get sweaty and cause hair loss. It is for that reason that so many kendo practitioners are bald.

ABOUT

This urban legend is particularly common amongst junior and high school students, where most kids will hear of it after joining the kendo club. Teenagers are especially concerned about their appearance, but for many who practice kendo, this doesn't become a real worry until they get older and notice that their hair is starting to get thinner. Was it kendo's fault after all?

This is a difficult question to answer. In most cases, probably not, but in some cases, perhaps the constant wearing of sweaty helmets *did* help speed the process along. A process that was going to take place anyway.

Kendo practitioners wear a large mask that covers their entire face to protect from blows. Inside that mask they place a towel to protect their forehead and soak up the sweat from wearing such a stuffy mask. The masks get incredibly hot, especially during the humid summer months, and training often lasts for several hours at a time. That can't be kind on anyone's hair, but does it really make you go bald?

A survey conducted by AGA Hair Clinic in 2017 revealed that men who were in the baseball or kendo clubs in high school were more likely to suffer hair loss as they grew older. Both sports involve wearing helmets for long periods of time, so obviously, the helmets are at fault, right? Not necessarily. A large part of it comes down to genetics and general health and hygiene. Plenty of baseball players, kendo practitioners, and in fact, anybody who spends long periods of time under a helmet, mask, or hat have zero problems with hair loss. However, bad hygiene and constant pulling on hair predispositioned to thin and fall out isn't going to help matters.

Keeping helmets clean and free of bacteria, as well as carefully washing and massaging hair after long, sweaty training sessions should be enough to keep from destroying your hair. Unless it's genetic, in which case, sadly no amount of washing is going to help, but that's not the helmet's fault either. At best, it might help speed hair loss up a little faster, but no hard research shows that simply wearing helmets for long periods of time causes baldness.

Human Body Anatomy Model

Schools all around the country have anatomic models of human bodies in their science rooms, but apparently some schools are using real dead bodies instead. These bodies are coated in preservatives so they don't rot.

ABOUT

It's a story you've probably heard yourself sometime. Maybe even seen in a horror movie once. That model of the human body in the science room that turns out to be not as lifeless as it seems. Or worse, there *was* life in it… once. It's not very believable that one could be an actual dead body though, is it?

In Japan, anatomy models for science rooms start from roughly 300,000 yen for a cheap model all the way up to one million yen for a top class one. This money has to come out of the school's pockets; they're not supplied for free. All schools are supposed to have one (although many may not, or they once did and it got wore down/destroyed/lost and they never replaced it), but that's a hefty chunk of cash for something that will only be used throughout certain lessons of the year. So, how can you save money on an expensive model of the human body? What if, maybe, just maybe…?

It sounds silly, but there is actually some truth to this horrifying legend, and much of this news has only come out recently. On December 6, 2018, a school in Kagoshima Prefecture discovered that the skull used as a model in the art room was actually a real woman's skull. They were unable to discover the identity of the woman, but the skull had been used in art lessons for over 20 years. This skull was only discovered because in June of the same year, another human skull was found in a different Kagoshima high school, leading to a prefecture-wide search for similar specimens.

On January 23, 2019, The Saga Board of Education revealed that human skulls and brains preserved in formalin were found in three schools under their jurisdiction as well. Police investigation revealed them to be real human remains, and while they did not believe there was any foul play at work, nobody knew how the schools got them. These were also found only because of the recent discoveries in other prefectures, leading many schools to check if their own science models and specimens were real or not. One of the schools involved said they had no idea they were dealing with real human remains. "We thought they were fake," they said. The remains had been in the schools for at least 20 years, so nobody knew where they came from. They were later taken by police to be disposed of.

On February 26, 2019, the Osaka Board of Education revealed they had received samples from 12 different schools that were thought to be real human bones and organs used as specimens in science classrooms. Another unnamed prefecture revealed that 14 of 199 schools had real human bones being used as skeleton displays, as well as various organs preserved in formalin. Most of these were thought to be obtained during the Taisho Era (1912-1926), but their exact origins were unknown.

On March 19, 2019, two high schools in Gunma Prefecture were found to have real specimens of foetuses, human bones, and kidneys. Again the police judged the specimens unlikely to be the victims of foul play, but they took them away to be cremated. These real-life models were found because a student who graduated from the school 40 years earlier contacted the Board of Education. She had memories of a real foetus being on display in the home economics room when she was at school. Which meant the specimens had been there for more than 40 years…

How did so many schools just happen to have real-life human specimens on display? One professor from Saga University suggested that numerous high schools around the country may have real human bones and organs because these were often sold to medical institutions during the Meiji and early Showa Eras (late 1800s to early 1940s).

And as for the Ministry of Education's thoughts on the matter? They were quoted as saying, "There are rules in place regarding the purchase and use of brain, skeleton, and human body anatomy models. When it comes to real life specimens, however, there are no rules because we did not assume that any were actually in use."

Whoops.

Mamushi Zake

A man who lived in Okinawa captured a *mamushi* (Japanese pit viper) and put it in a bottle full of strong shochu. He intended to make mamushi zake, a type of sake in which a mamushi is pickled in.

A few months later, the man thought it should be ready by now and opened the bottle. At that very moment, the mamushi sprang out of the bottle and bit him. The man was unable to fight the poison running throughout his body and soon died with the bottle of sake in hand.

It turns out that mamushi can live for up to half a year without food or water, which makes them incredibly hard to kill.

ABOUT

Mamushi, otherwise known as the Japanese pit viper, are extremely venomous and bite around 2000-3000 people in Japan each year. Of these, approximately 10 will die, while the rest require at least one week of treatment in the hospital, and in severe cases, intensive care. Mamushi are not to be taken lightly. They are, however, also used in many herbal medicines. Essence is extracted from their dried skins and organs and used in various health drinks you can buy anywhere.

In some cases, mamushi are also used with Japanese shochu to make mamushi zake. The dried skin and body are placed in a bottle of powerful shochu to pickle and add additional nutrients to the drink. Mamushi are incredibly powerful creatures and said to be difficult to kill, making them favoured for folk and herbal remedies. Mamushi zake is often used as a medicinal alcoholic beverage, and works to clear up bruises as well (as always, it's good to keep in mind that none of this has a scientific basis, being a folk medicine and all). Could it be true, then, that the above legend was or could be a real occurrence?

If a live mamushi is placed in a bottle of shochu, it's very possible for the snake to survive for at least a month. However, if one is planning to use a live mamushi and not a dried one, experts recommend using a high alcoholic content shochu, because there is a chance the snake will begin to rot. However, it's said that mamushi can survive for up to half a year without food or water, meaning that yes, there is a chance that if you bottle a live mamushi for several months and open it, that snake will still be alive and probably angry enough to bite you (which, let's be honest, you deserve if you're going to bottle a live animal in shochu just so you can drink its essence). Are you likely to die from it? Maybe. One in every 300 people bitten by a mamushi dies. The others end up in either extreme agony or, at the very least, a week long hospital visit. I don't like any of those odds, personally, and when vitamin drinks already exist with mamushi essence in them, why would you risk your life on it?

Death Necklace

One day, A, a high school girl, asked her friend B to show her the strange necklace she bought while on holiday overseas. She didn't know what type of jewel it was, but it shimmered with a bluish-white light. B was enthralled with it and often boasted about it to her. B started wearing the necklace every single day.

However, a few days later B suddenly stopped coming to school. Worried, A went to her house to see if she was okay.

"It seems I have a metal allergy," B told her, and looking closer, A could see the skin where her necklace sat was inflamed and peeling.

"I'm okay, it'll heal soon," B said, seeing A's worried face. A told her she would be waiting for her return at school, but B never showed up again.

About a month later, A suddenly got an email from B. *"Can you come over?"* A rushed over and was shocked by the sight before her. B had completely changed. She was skin and bones, most of her hair had fallen out, and her skin was turning a strange black tone.

A was speechless. With a shaking hand, B held something out towards her. "I want you to take this," she said. It was the shimmering necklace. "I don't need it anymore…"

Three days later, B died.

A was suspicious of the necklace B entrusted to her, so she took it to her uncle's jewelry store. The next morning, her uncle called her back, screaming and angry.

"How did you get your hands on something so dangerous?! This stone is crystallised uranium!"

That's right. Without knowing it, B had been constantly exposing herself to uranium, which eventually killed her.

ABOUT

There is a black market in Asia for "cooking" stones with radiation to give them a deeper, more illustrious colour that they otherwise wouldn't have. This can turn Chrysoberyl cat's eyes from pale yellow to a deep honey colour, or cheap light blue topaz into expensive dark blue topaz. These gems are then usually kept in a lead case until a certain period of time has passed and they're safe to release to the market, but sometimes less-than-scrupulous sellers may forgo that and release them into the wild immediately. Some of these make their way to Japan, and if they are released before they reach safe levels, can cause health problems down the line.

One jeweller from Bangkok discovered in 1997 that several cat's eyes he came into possession of had been hit with dangerous amounts of radiation to change their colour. He had already sold several to Hong Kong and Japan before discovering the truth, but officials stated that the amount of radiation discovered in them wouldn't be dangerous to society at large. He retrieved the stones and planned to put them in a lead box until they were safe for general sale.

This particular legend, however, is believed to be

inspired by the real-life Goiania accident which took place in Brazil in September 1987. Two men stole a small capsule of highly radioactive caesium chloride from an abandoned hospital and then sold it to a scrap yard. One of the thieves managed to pry into the canister to reveal a deep blue light. He then scooped some of it out. As the radioactive substances passed to the scrap yard, and then to another scrap yard, numerous people came into contact with it. In the end, four people died and 249 were contaminated. The incident was classified as one of the world's worst radiological incidents by the International Atomic Energy Agency.

Japan loves gemstones, just like any other country. Many come from overseas and, thanks to incidents like this, it's easy for outlandish stories to spread, particularly when one doesn't understand the precise details behind radiation and how it works.

Suicide by Tongue Biting

Amongst the many things we accept as reality from TV and movies, there is something that is just plain wrong.

In ninja movies and period plays you often see ninja who are captured bite their tongue to commit suicide, but that's just not possible.

ABOUT

If you watch old ninja movies or historical plays from Japan, you may have seen a scene like this before. A ninja gets captured and tied up so he can't escape, but any good ninja worth his weight in *shuriken* isn't going to let that keep him down. In order to protect his secrets, the ninja bites his own tongue off and promptly dies. It's similar to how Western movies would have you believe that twisting a person's head is enough to snap their neck and kill them instantly. The body doesn't really work like that, but it's seen so often that people start to believe it.

So, if you are captured by enemy forces, tied to a chair deep in a castle dungeon and unable to move any limbs, how are you going to end your life before the torture begins and they unearth all your ninja secrets? The answer, of course, is to bite off your own tongue and bleed to death. Like the instant death pill hidden inside a spy's tooth, all a good ninja needs is his teeth to end his own life. Bite down hard enough to cut your own tongue off, let the blood clog your throat, and you're off to the afterlife with all your secrets intact. Perfection. Except for the part where it's not.

In reality, it's extremely difficult to die simply by cutting or biting your own tongue off. Most people's gag reflex will see them soon coughing the blood up, and it's unlikely that the amount of blood loss from the tongue alone will be enough to end a life; especially not as quickly as it happens in ninja movies. If they are to be believed, then you'll be dead within a few seconds of biting; if not from blood clotting then from the remaining stump of your tongue curling back on itself and blocking your throat. Cue terrified children all over Japan when they accidentally bite their own tongue while eating. But, in reality, it just doesn't happen that way.

REAL-LIFE CASES

It's important to note that there *have* been documented cases in recent years of people attempting this method of suicide and succeeding, but *not* because of the tongue biting.

In 2003, a yakuza member in Fukuoka Prefecture was arrested for causing bodily harm, and while struggling with the police he bit his own tongue off. His official cause of death was strangulation whilst being subdued.

A 53-year-old artist in Shizuoka Prefecture was arrested on suspicion of murder on March 26 of the same year. While being questioned, the police noticed the man biting his own tongue and, fearing he was attempting to commit suicide, moved to transport him to a nearby hospital. The man was placed in a police wagon and reacted with violence. A towel was shoved in his mouth while he was held down with batons to stop him from further biting his tongue. He died on the way there. The official cause of death, however, was suffocation.

On January 6, 2018, a 55-year-old man being held at the Sapporo Chuo Police Station in Hokkaido was found convulsing after he screamed from his cell. He had bitten his own tongue. Officers attempted to resuscitate the man, but he was later pronounced dead at the hospital. The official cause of death was heart failure and had nothing to do with the man biting his tongue.

Yes, people technically have died after biting their tongues, but as in the above cases, this is generally because of another reason entirely; suffocation while being held down, or even unrelated heart attacks. It's just not possible to bite through your tongue and die within seconds like they portray in old ninja movies. You might still die, but it'll likely be for another reason. You can continue biting your tongue while chewing without fear of death!

ENTERTAINMENT

Peach Water CM Curse

Everyone has laid eyes upon it before. Suntory's Peach Water. You probably remember Kahara Tomomi's famous "hyuu hyuu" catch phrase. But did you know that, including Kahara, many of the entertainers who have promoted this drink over the years have ended up cursed, or even dead?

ABOUT

Suntory's Peach Water, or as it's known in Japan, Momo no Tennensui, is a drink first released by Japan Tobacco, or JT, in 1996. Production then moved to Suntory in 2015.

Also commonly known by the shortened names of Momosui or Momoten, it wasn't very popular when it first came out. As the product name implies, it is a natural spring water drink flavoured with peach juice; but unlike its competitors, which often have less than 1% juice to flavour their water, Peach Water uses as much as 10% peach juice in their flavouring.

In 1998, popular singer Kahara Tomomi (24 at the time) appeared in commercials for the drink uttering the now famous "hyuu hyuu" catch phrase—"hyuu hyuu" being the Japanese sound for exhaling or whistling. Sales for the drink went through the roof and it became a top seller for JT. However, there was a mould outbreak in some bottles used during the same year and the drink was forced to be recalled all over the country.

In 2015, the Peach Water brand was bought by

Suntory, and although production stopped shortly thereafter, at present you can still find the drink sold in stores and vending machines around the country.

So, how and why is it cursed?

CURSE OF THE PEACH WATER COMMERCIAL

Kahara Tomomi was the first entertainer to promote the peach-flavoured drink, but she wasn't the last, nor was she the only person to fall victim to its curse. Of all the singers and actresses that have promoted Peach Water over the years, many have fallen victim to illness, financial difficulties, and even death.

Kahara Tomomi seemed a natural fit to initially promote the drink. With her *tennen* (or airheaded) character, who better to promote "Tennenmizu"? Her catch phrase of "hyuu hyuu" while dancing around with a bottle of Peach Water stirred up sales countrywide.

Until that point, her own career had also been on the rise. Disaster soon struck, however. Kahara was going through a very public breakup with her producer, Komuro Tetsuya, much of which became fodder for the tabloids. Many of the rumours surrounding them involved drug abuse.

On January 17, 2009, Kahara was rushed to the hospital with acute medicinal poisoning. Doctors claimed it was an overdose from the large amount of tranquilisers she was on.

On January 30, less than two weeks later, Kahara was found passed out in her own house from gas poisoning. She claimed she was cooking yakisoba at the time, and her younger brother, who lived next door, discovered her. Many in the media assumed it to be a suicide attempt. Kahara had also just announced that she was in a new relationship, which the tabloids were jumping all over.

Dependent on sleeping pills and suffering from anaemia, her mental state was rapidly deteriorating. Kahara was eventually dismissed by her production company, and her time at the top was over.

In 1999, Hamasaki Ayumi took over and promoted the drink. Still a fresh-eyed newcomer to the music scene and gaining in popularity all over the world, Hamasaki was a smart choice for the peach-flavoured natural spring water looking for a new star to promote it.

In June 2000, however, Hamasaki suffered from an ear infection in her left ear. Against doctors' orders she continued performing, and in 2006 she was diagnosed with Ménière's disease. In January 2008, she announced that she had lost all hearing in her left ear. On May 20, 2017, she announced that she had started losing hearing in her right ear as well.

In 2000, a unit of three burgeoning idols was put together to promote the drink, consisting of Murata Yoko, Otani Mitsuho, and Yoshii Rei. Before long, Murata Yoko withdrew from promotions and was replaced with Kanbe Miyuki. Yoshii Rei then also withdrew and was replaced with Mitsuya Yoko. All five young women perfectly fit the image the drink was trying to promote, but regardless of their efforts, sales started to decline. Several of the women also seemed to fall victim to the Peach Water curse.

Murata Yoko, the first to withdraw, was fired by her agency in the same year, and she withdrew from show business. Rumors abounded that she had eloped with her manager, but when Murata eventually returned to the entertainment industry in 2003, she claimed she retired because of illness, suffering from chronic lower back pain.

Yoshii Rei, the second to withdraw, discovered the same year that she had acute myeloid leukemia. She received treatment for several months, and in 2001 received a bone marrow transplant from her mother. She suffered from graft-versus-host disease and lost 10 days' worth of memories after the transplant. It also changed her blood type from A to O and left her infertile. She returned to show business in 2002 with a best-selling book recounting her battle against leukemia, and in 2003 started acting again.

Kanbe Miyuki, who replaced Murata Yoko in the Peach Water trio, went on to become a well-known actress, model, and singer. However, her health started to fail in 2007, leaving her in and out of the hospital. On June 18, 2008, Kanbe passed away from sudden heart failure. She was 24.

Ohtani Mitsuho and Mitsuya Yoko, the other two members who promoted as part of the trio, have thus far escaped any of the ill-effects of the Peach Water curse.

In 2001, Peach Water wished to shift from a "cute" image to a "cool" image and Devon Aoki was employed to promote the drink. Commercials changed from cute dancing to a more stoic and laid-back approach. Aoki avoided the curse, but that didn't mean it was over.

In 2006, Kahara Tomomi came back to promote the brand once more in celebration of Peach Water going back to its original packaging. This also marked the 10th anniversary of Kahara's debut in show business. We know from earlier some of the awful things that happened to her after this second stint, including the cancellation of her contracts and various hospital visits.

In 2013, entertainer and model Rola appeared in commercials for the drink. Like Kahara, Rola was known as a *tennen* character on TV, making her a perfect fit for the brand. However, she too fell victim to the curse and in 2014, her father was arrested for health fraud. Although Rola had nothing to do with her father's actions, this affected her standing in the entertainment world nevertheless.

In 2018, weekly magazine *Shukan Bunshun* then revealed that Rola was locked into a 10-year "slave-like" contract with her agency and they wouldn't let her leave. Her television appearances decreased, as did her commercial contracts. Even her fanclub was suspended. It wasn't until April of the same year that Rola and her agency reached a settlement that allowed her to leave.

POWER OF THE PEACH

In Ancient China, it was thought the peach had powers to protect people from evil, and eating them would give long life. Peaches came to be viewed as talismans, or lucky charms, and that tradition transferred to Japan. In the Kojiki, Japan's oldest historical record, there is mention of the creator kami Izanagi throwing peaches at monsters to get rid of them. One of Japan's most famous fairy tales, Momotaro, features a boy born from a peach who goes on to kill many oni. So, if the peach is considered as a ward against evil, how did a peach-flavoured water come to be connected with a curse? Shouldn't it have the opposite effect?

The Chinese character for "peach" features in the Japanese word for utopia. In times of old, the peach was also likened to female genitalia. Female genitals were thought to be an earthly link to the underworld, so while the peach was revered for its demon-repelling powers, it was also viewed somewhat vulgarly as well.

If this earthly representation of the link to the underworld were made into a drink, like say, Peach Water, perhaps that drink might be a link to the other side as well. It's not a difficult conclusion to jump to when you notice a bunch of coincidences lining up, and hey, it makes for a good tale to tell your buddies.

CURSE OR COINCIDENCE?

Nine women have promoted Peach Water over the years, and only three haven't fallen victim to misfortune after filming their commercials. Was it truly just a coincidence, or something more sinister at work behind the scenes? That's up to you to decide, but Peach Water is still successfully selling throughout the country to this day, so at the very least, drinking it seems unlikely to send you to the underworld.

The Fan's Present

An idol held a fan event, and at the event she received numerous presents. Amongst those presents were several DVDs. They included B-grade horror movies, adult videos, and other such things. At any rate, she took all the presents home with her.

A few days later, the idol was drinking with her friend. As things started to calm down, she suggested they watch one of the DVDs her fans had given her. The idol's friend said they were probably just full of porn, but they had nothing else to do, so she agreed.

The idol put the DVD on and a male face appeared. He was doing the infamous *otaku* dance (the dance fans of idols perform to express their admiration). The idols friend burst out laughing at the sight.

"What the hell? That's so gross!" Yet the idol wasn't laughing. Her face turned pale, and her friend realised tears were running down her cheeks. "What's wrong?" she asked.

"That's… That's my room."

Looking closer, they could see the bed behind the dancing man. In the bed was the idol, blissfully unaware as she slept.

ABOUT

While it's likely that this legend has been around for quite a while longer, it was made popular when it appeared on the July 25, 2008 episode of *Yarisugi*

Cozy Urban Legend Special. The story, featuring gravure idol Minami Akina, was near word-for-word the story that's still passed around today. An idol receives a bunch of presents, takes them home, watches one of the videos and discovers that the fan filmed the video inside her house while she was lying there asleep.

While Minami acted in the short for the show, numerous fans contacted her afterwards to ask if the story was true. Minami posted on her blog on October 17, 2008, refuting that it was a real story involving her. "A lot of people have asked me whether that was a true story," she said. "It's not. I just appeared in the recreation, so don't worry. It's not about me." If the story wasn't about her, then who?

The idol system in Japan began in the 70s and hit its stride in the 80s. The scene exploded with manufactured singers who promoted, above all, innocence and wholesomeness. Idols were forbidden from public dating and had to maintain high morals at all times. A certain distance was kept between idols and their adoring fans, particularly in the time before social media. They were someone to look up to and worship, an image of purity, and as you can imagine, this created some pretty lop-sided relationships.

Around the early 2000s, this began to change with the introduction of social media, and in particular, the rise of handshake events where fans could directly meet and talk to their idols more frequently than in the past. Idols, once a symbol of the untouchable, became "the girl next door."

Anyone could buy a ticket, attend a handshake event, and directly talk to the girl of their choice. Do that enough times and they might even start to remember you.

The lop-sided relationship of the 80s and 90s began to morph. The image they sold of purity and wholesomeness remained, but if you spent enough money and went to see your favourite girl enough times, then maybe, just maybe, a real relationship could blossom. There have been numerous instances over the years of idols being caught out dating fans, so it's actually not that far-fetched to imagine.

In 2016, an unnamed idol was sued by her management company for breaking the "no dating" clause in her contract. She was discovered to be dating a fan, and they wanted 9,900,000 yen in damages. The case was thrown out by the Tokyo district court, who ruled that the clause was a breach of her basic human right to happiness. Is it unlikely that a fan will end up dating an idol? Of course. Is it impossible? Of course not. And that's all you need for dangerous situations to arise.

On December 8, 2018, two fans reportedly broke into an idol's home and attacked her. In light of the attack, which made worldwide headlines, several former idols came out and revealed similar situations where they were harassed or attacked in their own homes, and they're not alone.

In 2014, two members of a sister group were attacked by a saw-wielding fan at a handshake event.

In 2016, another idol was stabbed over 20 times

by a fan who was upset that she returned his gift.

In 2017, one idol spoke on TV about the numerous stuffed animals she received as gifts from fans. She was aware that they might have recording devices inside, and so she always hit them to make sure.

In 2018, members of a male dance troupe received a stuffed animal that had a GPS tracker inside, confirming that it is indeed a valid fear for idols to have. Shortly thereafter, idol group Batten Showjo-tai banned fan gifts entirely. The official reason was “they no longer had room to house the gifts,” but considering the dangers gifts often pose, it’s difficult to believe that as the only reason.

Idols, while presenting an image of constant availability in the current market, must also constantly be aware of the potential danger waiting around every corner, even in their own homes. This urban legend serves as a sobering reminder—as if real life weren’t enough of one—that danger can lurk anywhere, even if the safety of one’s home.

The Performer's Disappearance

A performer, A-san, went missing. His disappearance became news countrywide, but in reality A-san didn't disappear; he was kidnapped.

A-san went out fishing one night and happened to see people from a certain country kidnapping a Japanese person. Because he saw this taking place, A-san was taken as well. However, A-san's job meant that his name was well-known, and if he disappeared, it would become big news.

The kidnappers phoned someone to confirm that A-san was who he said he was, and once they did, told him, "If you tell anyone about what happened here today, even your family, you're dead." They returned A-san and then disappeared.

ABOUT

This urban legend is deliberately vague. The person is merely mentioned as being a performer, so they could be an actor, a singer, a comedian, or any mix of the above. That's not the important part of the story, however. The important part is that this person is famous, and they are kidnapped by "a certain country." That certain country is, no doubt, North Korea.

During the 1970s and 80s, North Korea kidnapped numerous people from Japan in order to teach Japanese language and culture to North Korean spies, as well as to steal their identities. The North Korean government admitted to these kidnappings in 2002, but were vehement that they were no longer taking place. It remains a sensitive issue, however, and many people remain fearful of potential abductions to this day.

But is there any truth to this rumour? It's not out of the realm of possibility to imagine that this could happen, and it's vague enough that nobody could say for certain that it didn't. If a famous person really was kidnapped by North Korea, it makes sense that people would want to keep that quiet. It turns out, however, that this urban legend *is* based on reality.

THE TRUTH

On March 3, 1991, Sugano Akinosuke, a performer who was famous for mimicking the singing style of Go Hiromi, went fishing off the coast of Atami City in Shizuoka Prefecture with five friends and family members. Sugano, who went by the performer's name of Wakado Akira and was 41 at the time, went for a walk alone at roughly 3 p.m. to a nearby breakwater to fish. His wife went to find him two hours later and discovered his fishing rod, hat, and glasses, but Sugano himself was nowhere to be seen.

Three days later he reappeared in Odawara City in Kanagawa Prefecture, about 20 kilometres away. A student discovered him lying face down close to Odawara Castle Park. Sugano claimed he had no memory of what happened to him during those three days, and the incident became news countrywide. According to the doctor who examined him, Sugano had taken a heavy blow to the head, which is likely what led to his amnesia. To this day, Sugano, who now performs under the name Gashuin Tatsuya, claims that he has no idea what happened during those three days, but the incident terrifies him.

Stories soon spread that the disappearance was all an act to make himself more famous. Sugano persisted that he had no idea what happened, which did nothing to dispel the rumours.

In 2003, however, the magazine *Shukan Shincho* proposed a different theory. They suggested that Sugano had instead seen someone being kidnapped by North Koreans, and when they realised this, they kidnapped him as well. In a panic, Sugano explained that he was famous, and if he went missing it would be all over the news. Not wanting to deal with the fallout of kidnapping someone famous, the kidnappers let him go with a warning that if he ever said anything, they would return and kill him.

When asked about this theory, Sugano responded, “There’s no way anything like that could be true.” Some found it strange that Sugano would refute the idea so strongly and immediately if he really had no memory of what happened. That’s something someone trying to hide the truth *would* say.

Conspiracy theories aside, unless Sugano ever comes out to say that yes, he was abducted, we’ll likely never know what really happened. The legend took on a life of its own, however, and there are still whispers of the famous “A-san” who was abducted by people from a “certain country” and told he would be killed if he ever revealed the truth of what happened.

Was he really abducted? Was it all a ploy for fame? Or was it something else entirely? Perhaps we'll never truly know, but isn't that what makes for the best urban legends?

The Former Idol's Verbal Slip

You may know Matsumoto Akiko as the host from the variety shows *Denpa Shonen* and *TV Champion*, and while she's often seen playing undesirable roles, did you know that she originally started out as an idol? Her fall from grace, however, stemmed from the infamous "Four Letter Incident."

Matsumoto was hosting a TV special when one of her male co-stars threatened to reveal her boyfriend's name on air. Revealing that she had a boyfriend would destroy her idol career, so of course she didn't want that to happen. Her co-star said, "If you want me to keep quiet, then say OOOO (slang for female genitalia)!" Matsumoto stood in front of the mic and said the word without hesitation. As a result, her television appearances dried up.

Several years later she returned on various variety programs, and now she retains consistent work. Instead of destroying her career, on the contrary, that four letter word helped propel her precarious idol career into a fully-fledged variety one.

ABOUT

Matsumoto Akiko, currently 52-years-old, is perhaps most famous for her appearances on variety shows and as an actress, and most people under 30 are probably unaware that she originally started her career as an idol. Idols in Japan have a pure image; they're forbidden to date and must always appear both available and sexually innocent. This urban legend is very much a reality, although the truth goes much deeper.

Born in Kagawa Prefecture in 1966, Matsumoto was 19-years-old when she appeared on live television with Kataoka Tsurutaro, a TV personality, and Shofukutei Tsuruko, a rakugo performer. It was a combined special between the shows *All Night Fuji* and *Shofukutei Tsuruko no All Night Nippon*.

At one point during the show, the men goaded her on-air with knowledge of her secret boyfriend. "I know who your boyfriend is. If you don't want us to reveal his name, then look at the camera and say OOOO. You'll become famous!"

The word they told her to say was slang for female genitalia, and being from Kagawa, Matsumoto was unaware of the word's meaning. Not only that, they claimed the man had once worked in Nichome, the infamous gay district of Shinjuku. She did as they said, fearful not just for herself but for her boyfriend if his name came out. Matsumoto was quickly escorted off-stage by security, unaware of what she had done wrong.

As a result of her live on-air utterance, Matsumoto was banned from appearing on Fuji TV, and her appearances on other channels also dwindled to zero. For two years this drought continued, with Matsumoto even sleeping in public toilets because she had no money.

One day, TV personality Nakayama Hideyuki, a performer from the same agency as Matsumoto, found her sitting on a bench near Kunitachi Station in Tokyo. She had been there all day. Nakayama had recently made his big break on the TV show *AB Brothers* and he asked her to join him doing variety shows instead. She took him up on the offer and Matsumoto's career was reborn.

On the August 13, 2013 episode of *Kaiketsu! Nainai Answer*, Matsumoto spoke of the "Four Letter Incident" on TV for the first time, nearly 30 years after the event. She revealed the men goaded her because her boyfriend, a male singer at the time, was bisexual. They said to her, "You don't want people to know you're dating someone gay, do you?"

On the January 25, 2016 episode of *Shikujiri Sensei Ore Mitai ni Naru na!*, she further revealed that she didn't just say the word once, but three times. Only one of these was actually broadcast, but it also happened to be a segment of the show that was being broadcast live on radio at the same time. Matsumoto revealed that the staffs' faces turned pale and security dragged her off without word. "I was born and raised in Shikoku, so I didn't know what the word meant," she said. "I had no problem with saying it at all."

Shofukutei, who was the main instigator of the incident, also found his work on TV dried up afterwards, although his career soon recovered. Both men claimed that they were just joking around and they thought that Matsumoto knew what the word meant. They didn't realise that she had no idea and would actually say it on-air.

Clips of the incident are still available on YouTube today, and it's clear that Matsumoto had no idea what she was saying. The two older men goad the young idol so much she is nearly in tears, crying for them to stop. They repeatedly manhandle her while threatening to, in essence, end both her career and that of her boyfriend's. It's not pleasant to watch.

After the incident, Matsumoto ended up breaking up with her boyfriend anyway, who was revealed to be Kato Shinta, a member of the band *Camelot*. Kato, who later came out as gay, no longer works in the entertainment industry, but he remains, unwittingly, the cause of one of the most shocking on-air utterances in Japanese television history.

Phone Wallpaper

They say that if you put a picture of Miwa Akihiro as your phone wallpaper for a week, your luck will rise. If he's wearing red clothes, your romantic fortunes will rise. If he's wearing yellow clothes, you'll have more luck with money.

ABOUT

Born in 1935, Miwa Akihiro is a Japanese singer-songwriter, actor, director, and author. He survived the nuclear bombing of Nagasaki during World War II and moved to Tokyo at age 17 to become a professional cabaret singer.

Well-known for his androgynous good looks when he was young, Miwa soon became a huge star and today remains one of the most well-known faces and names in Japanese entertainment. He has been critical of Japan's re-militarisation in recent years, being a survivor of Nagasaki and experiencing first-hand the horrors of war, but also outspoken about the Japanese people regaining their *bushido* (the samurai code of chivalry) and *Yamato-damashii* (the Japanese spirit).

So, how did he come to feature in this urban legend?

While the details remain unclear, this legend seems to have sprung to life thanks to a certain photo. In the photo, Miwa is wearing bright yellow clothes, his hair is bright yellow, and the set behind him is the same shade, from head to toe. Other than Miwa's face, everything is bright, almost fluorescent yellow.

In Feng Shui, yellow is the colour of wealth, so rumours began to spread that if you used this picture of Miwa as your phone wallpaper, your fortunes would rise. In addition, Miwa's face itself drew wealth to it. With his well-balanced face, wide forehead, carefree nose and ears said to bring good fortune, simply looking at Miwa was like "looking at the divine." Physiognomy, or face reading, is fairly popular in Japan, and it can tell one's fortunes, personality, and other traits merely by the shape of one's features. Apparently, Miwa was born to be wealthy.

Miwa wasn't the only subject of this legend, however. Other rumours suggested that if you used a picture of Tamori, a Japanese comedian known for always wearing sunglasses, you would be blessed with children.

Another said that if you used a picture of Matsuko Deluxe, another TV personality well-known for his poisonous tongue and cross-dressing stage persona, you would be blessed with good luck. It couldn't just be any picture, however. It had to feature Matsuko without any make-up and a shaved head, easily found by doing an image search. This legend was so widely spread that fellow celebrities such as actor Fukuyama Masaharu and members of the idol group AKB48 had him as their phone wallpaper.

More recent rumours have suggested that having a picture of comedian Hosei Tsukitei, perhaps best known as a regular from *Downtown Gaki no Tsukai*, would also bring good luck.

But why would using a photo of one of these celebrities as your phone wallpaper bring good luck? One theory suggests that they are used like modern day charms or amulets. Instead of going all the way to a shrine to buy one, it's much easier to change a phone wallpaper to a certain picture for a week and hope for the best that way. If you want wealth, seeing that bright yellow picture of Miwa every time you pick up your phone is likely to constantly remind you of it, and keep you focused on the goal: getting more money. Not only that, but perhaps simply having that picture there will be enough for the celebrities to share a bit of their luck with you. It doesn't have to make sense. People just need to believe in it for it to "work."

In 2012, Miwa himself commented on the legend. When asked on the program *Solomon Ryu* about whether there was any truth to the rumours that yellow pictures of him would bring wealth, and red pictures would bring luck in love, Miwa answered, "They're just rumours." It seemed the legend had also sent people Miwa's way when looking for advice in love, wealth, and other matters. "I'm not a fortune teller or a medium," he said, commenting that he was troubled by the amount of people coming to him for help.

If you really want to try for yourself, you can easily find the yellow picture in question by typing "Miwa Akihiro" into a search engine in English. And if you happen to become rich afterwards, let me know!

Matsushima Nahomi's Curse

It's said that a member of the popular comedic duo Othello, Matsushima Nahomi, has a curse placed upon her. That curse means that anything Matsushima likes will fall to misfortune. Singers, sports stars, actors, you name it. If Matsushima likes them, something unfortunate will happen to them. Those in the entertainment industry even call her the "White Devil."

ABOUT

Matsushima Nahomi, born in 1971 in Osaka, is a member of the comedic duo Othello. She works regularly on TV and is a face most Japanese people would be familiar with. She's also, apparently, cursed.

After a string of unfortunate events happening to those Matsushima publicly spoke of her fondness for, people started to joke that she was the "White Devil." The "white" in this case comes from her claim that she was the white piece from the game *Othello* while her comedic partner, Nakajima Tomoko, was the black piece.

But what evidence exists of this supposed curse? Let's take a look at some people Matsushima has liked over the years, and what befell them after her public announcements of support.

- Ozaki Yutaka (singer) → Died one month later in 1992, aged 26.
- Hide (singer) → Died one week later in

1998, aged 33.

- Judy and Mary (band) → Went on hiatus shortly thereafter, then disbanded in 2001.
- Hysteric Blue (band) → Guitarist Akamatsu Naoki was arrested in 2004 for rape. Group disbanded soon after.
- Orange Range (band) → Drummer Katchan left the group in 2005. They then released their last album in 2013 before going on a five-year hiatus.
- Hamanaka Osamu (baseball player) → Dropped as a Hanshin Tigers regular in 2007, then transferred to Orix Buffaloes, a much smaller team.
- Oshio Manabu (singer, actor) → Arrested for drug possession and neglect leading to a woman's death. Sentenced to 30-months in prison.
- David Beckham (soccer player) → Injured in 2010, kept out of World Cup.

A string of unfortunate coincidences, for sure. It would appear that Matsushima's curse extends not only to famous people, however.

- After buying her first horse race betting ticket for the horse Silence Suzuka, the horse broke its leg during the race and had to be put down.
- After announcing that she enjoyed K-1, a martial arts competition, the founder was arrested for tax evasion.
- After announcing she wanted to appear on

the TV show *Dash Village*, the *Dash Village* office was burnt down due to staff carelessness.
- As a child, at least five people a year killed themselves by jumping from the rooftop of the apartment building she lived in.
- A former boyfriend was arrested and sent to prison for fraud.
- When appearing on a radio program special about the supernatural, a ghostly face appeared in the window glass as she was laughing, scaring her manager so much that he quit.

But that's not all. This curse seems to extend even to her comedic partner, Nakajima Tomoko. In 2011, she was accused of not paying the rent on both her personal and business apartments, and she stopped showing up to work as well, hiding herself away from the world. The media reported that she was living with a female fortune-teller who had her brainwashed. This fortune-teller supposedly drove a wedge between Nakajima and Matsushima, keeping them apart as Matsushima's popularity rose to new heights while Nakajima's faltered. Othello was disbanded in 2013, but Nakajima slowly started to make her comeback in the entertainment industry as a solo performer thereafter.

In 2015, she claimed on *Downtown Now SP* that she wasn't brainwashed, nor was she living with the fortune-teller. Instead, she didn't have a written contract with her company and they were increasingly in disagreement about their management policies. She didn't know how to leave them, so she stopped going to work so they would fire her. The fortune-teller was simply a friend, and they didn't live together. The truth may never be known, but it remains another notch on Matsushima's long list of associated curses.

There's no denying that numerous unfortunate events have happened to those Matsushima has given her public support to over the years. Is it really a curse? I don't believe in curses myself, so I'm more inclined to say it's a long series of unfortunate events that could easily be misconstrued as something else. It no doubt makes for an interesting story at parties though!

Death Blog

Higashihara Aki, a model for Platinum Productions and wife of Olympic athlete Inoue Kosei, also runs her own popular blog on Ameba. However, the topics she posts about are soon followed by misfortune, so much so that her blog has come to be known as the "Death Blog."

ABOUT

Higashihara Aki first debuted in 2003 as a model for Asahi Beer. Over the course of her career she's modelled for various magazines and fashion lines, as well as worked on TV as a newscaster and personality. She also runs her own blog on the popular Japanese Ameba website, which is still actively updated today. It wasn't long, however, before her blog became infamous for the seemingly strange coincidences that followed her posts. Whenever Higashihara posted about a topic, it wouldn't be long before something terrible happened to that person, place, or event. Here are some examples of topics she blogged about and the misfortune that followed shortly thereafter.

- Myojinmaru Food CM → Their Cup Yakisoba line was found to be infested with bugs.
- Mentioned that Chinese stocks seemed to be on the rise → The stocks crashed.
- Worked as chairman for the Birdman Contest → The starting area was destroyed

by a sudden squall while being dismantled.

- Worked as an assistant for the Birdman Contest → The contest was cancelled.
- Went on a trip to Korea → Korean won fell.
- Announced plans to study in England → English pound fell.
- Posted a photo of a pizza from Saizeriya, an Italian restaurant chain → A toxic chemical was discovered in their frozen pizzas.
- Went to England → Queen Elizabeth revealed to have lost 37 million pounds in just a few weeks due to the financial crisis.
- Announced her support for Peter Aerts, a Dutch kickboxer → Lost to Bard Hari.
- Went to the wedding of Fujiwara Norika and Jinnai Tomonori → They divorced.
- Posted about how the new terrestrial digital broadcasting logo was annoying and "in the way" → Kusanagi Tsuyoshi, the model and spokesperson for the change from analogue to digital TV, was arrested.
- Recommended the comedic duo Joyman → Soon involved in a scandal and lost popularity.
- Dreamt of Sakai Noriko, a popular singer → Sakai was arrested on suspicion of possessing and using drugs.
- Blogged about Sky Tree → Elevator failed on opening day.
- Went to a McDonalds event → Bugs were found in food in US restaurants.
- Blogged about the snack Umaibou → Umaibou factory caught on fire.

- Appeared in CMs for finance and loan company DIC → Company closed all stores.
- Acted as campaign girl for Asahi Beer → Asahi dropped from first place in beer sales.
- Participated in a penny auction → Complaints rose about unfair practises.
- Wondered if Michael Jackson would take his tour to England → Michael Jackson passed away.
- Bought an iPad → Steve Jobs fell seriously ill.
- Announced she would be landing in Miyazaki Prefecture → Shinmoedake erupted, disrupting traffic.
- Announced her support of "blog rival" Ogura Yuko → Ogura's ramen store caught on fire.
- Announced she was spending time with a family she met on Japanese social media website Mixi → Mixi's servers went down for a long period.
- Blogged about how swings (*buranko*, or *blanko*, in Japanese) were scary at night time → Baseball player Tony Blanco broke a bone that same night.
- Randomly mentioned that even pandas neglect their children sometimes → The next day, Ueno Zoo announced the death of their baby giant panda.
- Promoted JINS glasses → The company was hacked and people's credit card information stolen.
- Went to Tokyo Disneyland → The next day

they suffered their very first accident when a safety bar wouldn't go down and a man was injured.

- Remarked her daughter was mimicking comedian Sugichan → Sugichan suffered a thoracic spine fracture that took three months to heal.
- Posted about Tokyo Dome → The next day, Yomiuri Giants (whose home stadium is Tokyo Dome) lost the championship.
- Mentioned watching Crayon Shin-chan on DVD → Creator Usui Yoshito passed away.
- Posted a photo of a toy plane her son was playing with → Two weeks later, the newly introduced Boeing 787 line was found to have several faults. One plane suffered from an electrical fire on board and was forced into an emergency landing. The entire fleet ended up being grounded.

At this point, you would think that Higashihara should probably stop blogging entirely. This isn't even the entirety of the strange coincidences readers of her blog have noticed, but it gives you a good idea of why it came to be somewhat affectionately known as the "Death Blog." It may seem reminiscent of Matsushima Nahomi's curse, where anybody she publicly supports soon suffers a terrible fate. In fact, this pair have been called by some the Devil of the East (Higashihara in Tokyo) and the Devil of the West (Matsushima in Osaka).

Unsurprisingly, Higashihara herself is aware of what people call her blog, and has spoken on TV about how it's often on her mind. Her blog reached peak infamy around 2013 due to a rapid string of incidents, but now, around 10 years after she first started writing, things seem to have calmed down.

Still, people must undoubtedly get nervous when they see their names pop up in one of her posts. You never know what might happen…

Dragon Ball GT's Meaning

Dragon Ball GT hit the airwaves in 1996 and aired for close to two years. However, despite its popularity, nobody could ever fully explain what "GT" really stood for.

In reality, *Dragon Ball GT* was made without any help from Toriyama Akira, the original creator, and so the company producing the show added "GT" as an apology to him. It actually stood for *Gomen ne* (sorry) *Toriyama-sensei.*

ABOUT

This legend could easily fit in the joke section as well. *Dragon Ball GT* was generally not very well received by fans when it was originally released. It was a new story created not by Toriyama Akira, the creator, but by TOEI Animation, the company behind the anime adaption of his original work. When *Dragon Ball Z* ended, TOEI approached both Toriyama and *Shuukan Shonen Jump*, the magazine which published *Dragon Ball*, and informed them of their desire to make a new show that continued 10 years after the battle with Majin Buu. Both Toriyama and his publisher agreed and even gave their own ideas for the show, and in the end it was Toriyama himself who gave the show its title of *GT: Grand Tour*, not *Gomen ne, Toriyama-sensei.*

Needless to say, there's not much truth in this one.

The Idol's Prediction

This happened a long time ago, on the TV show *Neruton Benikujira Dan*. On this particular day, popular singer Nakamori Akina appeared as a guest. One of the hosts asked her a simple question.

"What type of man do you like?"

Nakamori responded, "I like men like Miyazaki Tsutomu."

She had meant to say Yamazaki Tsutomu, a popular actor, and instead said "Miyazaki."

A few days later, news of a man who was arrested for crimes that shook the world was announced. His name was Miyazaki Tsutomu, the Little Girl Murderer.

ABOUT

Nakamori Akina is a popular singer who is still releasing albums to this day. She debuted at age 16 when she won the 1981 season of talent show *Star Tanjo!*, and has to-date sold over 25,340,000 albums, making her the third best-selling idol in Japan's history (behind SMAP and Matsuda Seiko). Nakamori was at the pinnacle of her career when she was scheduled to appear on the talk show *Neruton Benikujira Dan* in 1989. That year would prove to be the darkest of Nakamori's life, for various reasons.

Nakamori was scheduled to appear on *Neruton Benikujira Dan* for its June 17, 1989 episode. However, when Nakamori's interview segment was due to air, the screen suddenly cut off and switched to a "Please wait a moment" placard. The program continued to flicker in and out, before finally going to black with the text "Due to breaking news, this program has been cancelled. Please understand." The program then cut to a commercial, but scenes of Nakamori's interview continued to cut in and out. Finally the screen turned to colour bars, and the show ended.

A few days later, the episode was rescheduled. A notice was put up before the show announcing "We apologise that the June 17 episode of *Neruton Benikujira Dan* was cancelled. We will air it now." This time, the episode proceeded as normal. The hosts asked Nakamori what type of man she liked.

"A man with a nice smile," she answered.

"Can you give us an example using a famous person?" they asked.

"Miyazaki Tsutomu," she answered. The hosts were briefly confused, because there was no famous person with that name.

"You mean Yamazaki Tsutomu?" they clarified. "Come on, at least get his name right!"

Nakamori, confused, then said, "Huh, I don't know why, but inside my head I always thought it was Miyazaki."

At the time, Nakamori was publicly dating fellow singer Kondo Masahiko. They briefly spoke about her relationship with him and the show ended. People soon forgot about the strange hiccup that kept the show off the air and moved on. A few weeks later, breaking news revealed that a man named Miyazaki Tsutomu had been arrested for sexually assaulting and murdering several young girls. The very same name Nakamori had said was her "ideal type" on the TV program that suffered technical difficulties, proclaimed it was being interrupted for breaking news (when there was none, at least, not at that time), and then had to be rescheduled for a later date. A strange coincidence, to be sure, but things got even stranger.

As mentioned earlier, 1989 was a troubling year for Nakamori. Her relationship with Kondo was on the rocks, and there was talk that her hit single "Liar" was written about him. On July 11, just a few weeks after her appearance on *Neruton Benikujira* Dan aired, Nakamori cut her left wrist inside Kondo's apartment in a suicide attempt. She was found and taken to the hospital in time, but the news shocked Japan. Then, less than two weeks later, Miyazaki Tsutomu was arrested.

The strange coincidences went even further than that. While Nakamori recovered, both mentally, physically, and career-wise, Miyazaki Tsutomu, the Little Girl Murderer and man whose name she had mistakenly said was her ideal type on TV, was sentenced to death. He was executed on June 17, 2008. The exact same date Nakamori's original interview was supposed to air. The same date it was besieged with technical difficulties, strange warnings of breaking news, and then finally cancelled.

Makes you think, doesn't it?

Jungle

Did you know that in 1992, two different commercials were aired late at night that had subliminal messages? These commercials were called "Jungle" and there were two versions; a doll version and a heart version.

The doll version featured a song that strongly resembled the national anthem, *Kimi Ga Yo*. A doll appeared on screen, and with each flash of light the number of dolls multiplied. The lyrics sang of the pain of life and death, and as the flashes extended, the dolls appeared to die in pain like victims of an atomic bomb. It then ended with a voice screaming painfully, "Come on then, look!"

The heart version featured a healthy-looking pink heart (the shape, not an actual heart). The colours of the heart flashed in and out and slowly it decayed until rotten. If you traced over the dark, rotten spots, it spelt out "AIDS." Right after the commercial began, a needle stabbed the upper right portion of the heart, signifying it was dying because of infection from a used needle, highlighting the horrors of drugs.

ABOUT

Although they're not commercials, the videos mentioned in this legend *are* real and you can still watch them on the internet today. They are admittedly pretty creepy. The shorts were actually eye-catches; short clips used to begin and end commercial breaks on Japanese TV. They aired during Fuji TV's late night programming block called Jungle, which aired from October 1992 to September 1993.

The short clips, which both featured 15 and 30 second versions, were supposed to set the mood for the late-night block. The heart version aired on Tuesdays, Thursdays, and Saturdays, while the doll version aired on Mondays, Wednesdays, Fridays, and Sundays. Although they were never commercials, nor were they aiming to sell anything, the imagery was so vivid that people still remember them today *as* commercials.

Not long after the shorts started to air, people began murmuring about the supposed subliminal messages hidden inside them. They were called the "weird" commercials, the "fear" commercials, the "mysterious" commercials. Why did the rotten heart spell out AIDS? Why were dolls writhing in pain under what looked like an atomic bomb flash?

THE TRUTH

The head of editing at Fuji TV at the time was Ogawa Shinichi. When it came time to create the eye catches for the late-night programming slot, he reportedly said, "Anything goes. Mix it all up!" By mixing several elements together, they would end up with something strange and mysterious, which was his goal and also the reasoning behind the name "Jungle."

According to the creators who worked on the short clips, there were no hidden meanings behind them. They were created to demonstrate and wild freedom and abandonment the Jungle late-night programming was supposed to offer. Anything goes, after all! It's hard to argue after seeing the clips that they didn't do a good job of setting the mood, if nothing else.

So, the official line was that there was no message behind either video. Of course, even if the creators did try to hide subliminal messages in the clips, it's unlikely they'd come out and admit that, even several decades later.

There's no denying that the commercials were designed to push people's buttons so they would be remembered, and it's hard to deny that they were playing on the very real fear of both AIDS and nuclear bombing. Whether they were supposed to be anything other than memorable, however, we'll likely never know.

Severed Head on Live Broadcast

This happened on the TV show *Totsuzen Gabacho*, an old program that featured comedian Shofukutei Tsurube.

The hosts were discussing a ghost photo they had received in which three women appeared to be missing body parts; arms, legs, and even a head. Of the three women in the photo, two of them were already dead. Their limbs were severed when they died. The final woman, the one missing her head, was still alive. It was this woman who sent the photo in to the program because she feared it was cursed, and she would be next.

The program invited the woman to appear so they could prove the curse wasn't real. It was a late night live program, so the woman's mother accompanied her to the studio. However, right as they arrived, the woman was hit by a car and her head cut off. The mother, shocked and confused, picked up her daughter's still bleeding head and carried it upstairs to where the show was filming live.

People inside the studio screamed when they saw her, and for just a second the severed head appeared on camera before they panicked, swung the camera to the roof, and then turned it off entirely. It was only a few seconds, but this footage was broadcast all over the Osaka area. Thanks to that, the program was thereafter cancelled.

ABOUT

Totsuzen Gabacho was a variety program that aired from October 5, 1982 to September 24, 1985. It ran in the 10 p.m. slot for an hour and occasionally featured a corner where the hosts shared scary stories, ghost photos, etc. And, if you believe the legend, also once aired live footage of a woman's severed head.

There was a period where if you typed "Shofukutei Tsurube" into a search engine in Japanese, one of the first suggestions that would show up would be "severed head." Other more pertinent news has booted that term out of the list recently, but that's how popular this urban legend was, and continues to be.

But is there any truth to it? Did a woman really send in a cursed photo, only to die on her way to the studio to prove it wasn't real and have her shocked mother carry the head on stage before a live TV audience?

THE TRUTH

You don't have to dig too far to discover that this legend is just that. No such photo ever appeared on the show, no such woman was ever invited, and despite people going back through all the final episodes of the show—which was supposedly cancelled after this incident took place—nobody ever found anything even remotely resembling what happens in this story.

Thinking about it rationally, the story itself

already seems unlikely. How would a woman manage to carry the severed head of her daughter all the way up to a live studio broadcast from outside the building without anybody seeing or stopping her? Like most television programs in Japan, the studios are located in large skyscrapers in the city and people need to get through a variety of receptions, elevators, and security before they can get to where they're going. It's extremely unlikely that this would ever occur, but even if we suppose that every single person was asleep that night—because it was a late night broadcast after all—and not a single person managed to capture it on tape as it aired, there is another reason we know this story to be fake: the creator of it came out and said as much.

On February 18, 2001, Shofukutei appeared on *Saigo no Bansan* and spoke publicly for the first time of the rumours. He straight out denied that anything of the sort had ever happened. "How did such an outrageous story even come about?" he said. "I could understand it if they made the story up about someone scarier than me, but it goes entirely against my character!"

Japanese television personalities have certain traits and characteristics they portray, much like an actor playing a role (for example, the airhead, the angry woman, the womaniser, etc), and Shofukutei was a comedian. He was the funny guy. Why would people try to use him as the basis for a scary urban legend? It would be more believable if it were a personality who was known for being darker, basically.

It turns out there was a good reason for it being Shofukutei, however. At the same time *Totsuzen Gabacho* was running, Shofukutei also hosted a radio program called *Nukarumi no Sekai*. For some unknown reason, a listener of that show created the story and shared it. Here's where it gets a little muddy, because there are also versions of this legend that don't involve *Totsuzen Gabacho* at all, but instead it was said to happen while Shofukutei was hosting *Nukarumi no Sekai*. That version goes as follows:

When Shofukutei Tsurube was working as a DJ on radio, he received a letter from a listener.

"I went on holiday with three of my friends and had a stranger take a photo of us. A short while later our friend sent the picture to all of us, but apparently, we were all headless in it. After that, the friend who sent me the photo and the two others died in accidents. I'm the only one left! I'm not brave enough to look at the photo myself, what should I do?"

Worried, Shofukutei called the woman directly.

"I looked at it! I'm gonna die!" The woman was in a panic.

"If you're that worried about it, bring the photo to me right now," Shofukutei said. The listener agreed, and the program continued.

However, after a long commercial break, Shofukutei could be heard crying. The woman he had spoken to earlier on the phone had died on her way there.

"It's my fault. I did this..." Shofukutei's voice echoed lifelessly from the speakers.

It's likely that this version of the legend was the original, and the creator of the story admitted that it was something they made up. Over time, embellishments were added and somehow the woman without a head in the photo actually lost her head in an accident on the way over. The radio program was changed to the television program Shofukutei was appearing on at the same time, and an extra grizzly bit of horror was added to the end. The woman didn't just die, her mother carried her severed head all the way up to the program and it appeared on live TV. Admittedly, this is far more gruesome and horrifying than the radio version, which is also likely why it's the most popular version today.

So no, there was never a severed head live on late night television. Just an imaginative story that took on a life of its own and grew to be a horrifying legend still talked about nearly 40 years later.

Mysterious Vinyl String

Tantei! Knight Scoop started airing in 1988, and even today it remains a popular TV program in the Kansai area. They investigate all sorts of requests from listeners, and for 20 years now they've been sending out comedians and entertainers to discover the truth behind these stories.

However, in all these years the show has been on the air, there has only been one investigation that they halted and decided not to pursue any further.

The year was 1992. People were discovering numerous vinyl strings attached to guard rails and telephone poles around Konoikeshinden in Osaka. Nobody knew what they meant. Finding it strange, the public requested *Tantei! Knight Scoop* to investigate. Kitamura Masahide, better known as TOMMY's Masa, one half of a popular manzai duo, was dispatched to check it out.

He discovered the strings tied in various places around town, and even while he was investigating the number of strings grew. Only ten minutes had passed since he last investigated and returned to find even more, setting the members back in the studio on edge. In the end he discovered that a pole behind a particular gas station was covered in countless strings, causing studio members to scream in horror.

However, at the end of the episode, a note was displayed signalling an end to the investigation, and the program wouldn't be taking any further tips from the public. Many suggested the strings were just leftovers from signs hung in the area, but locals said they'd never seen any signs there before.

After the show, members of the local government collected all the strings, and nobody ever found out why they were there to begin with. In reality, however, the show discovered who really put the strings there. When they asked her why, she answered, "I don't know why… I just had to."

ABOUT

Tantei! Knight Scoop first aired on March 5, 1988, and is still on the air today. It's a variety program where various comedians work together as a "detective agency" and take on requests from viewers to get to the bottom of things. The show is based in Osaka, but they venture out into other areas of Japan when necessary. This particular episode featuring the mysterious vinyl strings aired on March 20, 1992. The "detective" was TOMMY's Masa, who was dispatched to Konoikeshinden in Osaka after the show received a letter from a troubled clothing store owner. That letter was as follows:

I run a clothing store in Higashi Osaka City. I'm writing to you because there is something I hope you can investigate promptly.

Starting several weeks ago, I noticed that something like a yellow string had been tied to the telephone pole in front of my store. At first I wasn't concerned by it, but every morning when I look at it, the number of strings has multiplied. At first I thought it was just in front of my store, but looking closer I realised the strings are tied everywhere. Moreover, in front of my store is particularly bad.

It's constantly on my mind. Who tied these strings, and for what purpose? Could you please investigate for us?

This letter was introduced at the start of the episode. Somebody was tying strings around town, and nobody knew why. Not only that, but the numbers were increasing as time went on, making the residents feel uncomfortable and unsettled. Who was doing this, and why?

INVESTIGATION

The shop owner ran a store called SAURUS. When Masa went out to investigate, he saw the vinyl strings attached to the telephone pole first-hand. According to the owner, they had been tied there two or three weeks earlier. At first the strings were yellow, but after that, blue strings were added. It turned out he discovered red strings tied behind the store as well, and as recently as the day before, white strings.

Both the store owner and Masa were understandably unnerved by these strange events. Thinking to lift a fingerprint from the strings, Masa called the local police station. He was surprised to discover that the police already had an officer in charge of dealing with the string incidents, and he was put through to him directly. Masa attempted to explain the fear residents were feeling and wondered if they could get a fingerprint from the strings. The officer came out to meet him, but explained that tying strings to poles wasn't a crime so there wasn't much they could do about it.

After further investigations, Masa discovered the strings covered almost the entire area near Konoikeshinden Station. He attempted to remove a yellow string from a gymnastics bar in the park and discovered it was tied twice in a hard knot. He could determine no pattern to their placement around town either. They appeared to be entirely random.

Next, he called the local city hall. Once more he was put through to someone in charge of the string incidents; the random strings around town were so prolific that both the police and city hall had people in charge of dealing with them. The person in charge informed Masa they also had no idea what was going on, but he did confirm they weren't being used as signs for construction work.

Masa then went to a local stationery store to uncover whether they'd sold a lot of vinyl string recently. The owner confirmed they were out of yellow because someone had recently purchased them all, while other colours were low on stock for the same reason. Whoever the perpetrator was, it was likely they bought the string from that very store, but the owner had no idea who it might have been.

Shortly thereafter, the police went around town taking all the vinyl string down. Nobody knew when it might return though, and the fear that they would be back soon remained. Masa continued his investigations and discovered the end of the stringed areas was a telephone pole in front of a gas station near the Kusumibashi intersection. There were no strings past that point, and the pole itself was covered in what appeared to be hundreds of blue strings.

After speaking to the gas station attendant, he revealed that they even found strings tied to their car wash. They were tied there about two or three months earlier. Masa joked that they were cursed, but the staff claimed it didn't bother them because nobody was getting hurt.

And that marked the end of the investigation. Masa mentioned it was the strangest case he'd ever worked on, and a note appeared at the end of the show:

End of Investigation

We will no longer be receiving information related to this case. Please understand.

POSSIBLE EXPLANATIONS

As the urban legend states, this is the only investigation the program ever put a stop to, and no reason was given as to why. After airing the episode, it was brushed under the rug and never spoken of again, even though it was clearly unsolved. This sent the rumour mill into overdrive.

One theory was that the strings were leftover from signs hung on poles. These signs did use the same string, but a single glance at the number of strings was enough to put that rumour to rest. Some poles were densely packed with them, more strings than people could count, and as the residents themselves said, they couldn't recall ever seeing signs there. That idea was out.

Kamioka Ryutaro, a comedian on the show, suggested that maybe the strings made an image when viewed from the sky. In later years on the internet, people chimed in that perhaps the mysterious strings were some sort of spiritual barrier, and that the image was protecting Osaka. However, Masa mapped all the strings he came across and no discernible image could be seen. Whether they were random or not, they *looked* random and didn't make any recognisable picture.

The final theory was that the show *did* uncover the perpetrator… but that person was unfit for broadcast. It didn't take long for people to start putting two and two together, and the general consensus was that this was the most likely reason. Why else would they air an investigation, only to abandon it at the end? The show always got to the bottom of its viewer requests, so it was odd that this one was called off.

But was it really? If the show had found the culprit, but the person was perhaps mentally ill, they would be unable to put that on air. Instead, they announced an end to the investigation, and that was that.

THE PERPETRATOR

In 2006, video of the original episode was shared online, bringing the mysterious unsolved legend back to the public's mind. Someone who claimed to be a local that appeared in the background of the original *Tantei! Knight Scoop* episode posted that he had seen the person tying strings to poles on his way home from school. It was dark, however, so he couldn't see the person very well.

A few years later, in 2012, an anonymous poster claimed that his friend pointed a woman out and called her the "String Lady." Another poster shared that the show abruptly ended investigations because in reality they *had* discovered the person tying the strings, and she was mentally handicapped. Supposedly, she tied the strings so she didn't get lost while she was out walking, and that was why they grew in number day by day, so they stood out.

In 2015, another person claiming to be a local also posted that it was an unemployed woman with a mental disability. She was seen walking around town holding rolls of string, most often in the early morning. Because she looked like a regular housewife out to do some shopping, nobody ever suspected her of anything.

A story also began to spread that when the police asked the woman why she did it, she answered with "I don't know why, I just have to." The internet being what it is, there is no proof that the perpetrator actually was a mentally handicapped woman to begin with, nor that she was ever arrested, nor that that was her response to theoretical police questioning.

Tantei! Knight Scoop has never said anything further about the case, so officially, it ended in mystery. The internet, never happy to let a mystery go unsolved, supposedly uncovered the culprit, and as the best conspiracy theories go, it seems like it *could* be the truth. Is it? Perhaps we'll never know, but for now, it's the strongest unofficial answer that we have.

JOKES

Rhinoceros Beetle

"Mum, do we have any batteries?" a young boy asked his mother.

"I think there are some in the bottom drawer," she replied. "What do you need them for?"

"Um, my Rhinoceros beetle stopped moving, so I'm gonna change its batteries," the boy answered with a smile.

Kids these days don't have many chances to interact with nature, and so there are many children who make small misunderstandings like this.

ABOUT

Though it might seem more recent, this urban legend has been around since at least the 1980s. The story itself is pretty straight-forward, but this particular joke came about because of the worry that children were spending too much time with technology and not enough time outside with nature. All the boy knows is technology, so when his pet beetle dies, he assumes it just needs a change of batteries. Bug catching is still a hugely popular pastime with Japanese kids today, however, so it seems unlikely that any are going to confuse a real bug for a robot toy anytime soon.

Blue Urine

One day, a nappy company received a phone call from a distraught mother.

"How can we help you, ma'am?"

"I'm sorry, but my child's urine is yellow! Your commercials showed it to be blue, so I'm a little worried..."

ABOUT

We may laugh, but there seem to be people out there who, perhaps due to a lack of general education, believe that babies' urine is supposed to be blue, and that it turns yellow over time. By the same token, there are some men who (apparently) believe that women's menstrual blood is also blue thanks to these commercials.

Of course, blue is used in diaper commercials not because it resembles the actual colour of the liquid coming out, but because blue is easy to see against white. Your baby's yellow urine is perfectly fine, and if your menstrual blood is blue, well, you'll probably want to see a doctor about that.

There is a real disease called "blue diaper syndrome," however, which is a rare metabolic disorder that can cause a baby's urine to stain their diaper blue. It is an unfortunate coincidence that has nothing to do with why commercials use blue liquid to show off their diapers' soaking power.

There have been calls from some corners of the Japanese internet to change the colour of the liquid used in commercials to help avoid this confusion.

The argument being that some people don't have the support of other parents or family members around them, and so learning that their newborn baby doesn't pee blue can be distressing. Considering the information age we now live in, and how it takes only a few seconds of research to discover that "hmm, my baby's yellow urine is perfectly fine," these calls haven't been taken very seriously.

A Brother's Jealousy

One day, a young boy discovered he was about to become an older brother. He had lived his life happy and free until that point, but once his young brother was born, he realised that his parents would devote all their time to him instead.

And so they did, and the boy grew angrier and angrier, until finally his parents told him off. "You're an older brother now, grow up!"

The boy made plans to kill his baby brother instead. His brother was always suckling from their mother's breast, so if he could somehow coat it in poison, that would solve his problem.

The boy got to work right away. Once his younger brother was dead, he would get all the attention again. However, the following day something unexpected happened.

It wasn't his younger brother that died. It was his father.

ABOUT

If you didn't laugh at this one, you're a better person than I am. This joke has been circulating for at least a few decades now, and oftentimes includes a variation where it isn't the father who dies from suckling on the mother's poisoned breast, but the next-door neighbour instead… Whoops.

Another version, which you may have heard before, tells of a baby that says a name each day, and the very next day that person dies. Much in the same vein as this tale, the twist comes at the end when the baby says "father" and it's the next-door neighbour who dies. Whoops.

These are somewhat similar to the "milkman" stories we share in the West. Japan doesn't have a history of milkmen, so the joke doesn't translate well, but adultery with a neighbour is universal.

The Hairdresser's Customer

A hairdresser close to the station was closing up shop for the day. It was a little early, but the young woman was the only person there, so she began closing up.

Right at that moment, a businessman burst into the store. The woman informed him that they were closing for the day, but the man said he had an important meeting the next day and he needed his hair cut immediately.

The hairdresser relented and covered the man in a sheet. She then went out the back to grab her tools. On her way back, the woman saw something unbelievable. The man's hand was moving frantically underneath the sheet near his crotch.

The woman was alone and, suddenly fearful, she threw her tools at the back of the man's head. The man passed out, and the hairdresser fled to the nearby police box. The police accompanied her back to the store and when they removed the sheet from the unconscious man, they discovered the man's glasses and handkerchief sitting beside him.

The man had been cleaning his glasses.

ABOUT

Perhaps you've heard an urban legend extremely similar to this one. It often goes by the name "The Hairdresser's Error" overseas, and it's believed this legend originated in the late 1970s. This is one of the few legends that made its way to Japanese shores and remained almost wholly unchanged.

This story is still shared around Japan today, particularly amongst beauticians and those training to be hairdressers.

There's also a similar legend that takes place on a plane:

> During a flight, a cabin attendant noticed a man's hands moving underneath his blanket. The movements seemed suspicious, so she went to her superior and alerted him as to what was going on. They went to check on the man together and, as expected, his hands were still moving in rubbing motions under the blanket.
>
> "Excuse me, sir, but what are you doing?" the superior asked in a strong tone of voice. The man looked back at them absentmindedly.
>
> "Is there something wrong with fixing my camera mid-flight?"
>
> The man removed his hands from under the blanket to reveal a camera that he was holding tightly.

Sometimes a funny story crosses all cultures and even jobs.

General Offensive

During the war, roughly 400 members of the Imperial Army found themselves besieged on an island. They were surrounded by the Americans.

The Japanese soldiers abandoned their base on the shore and made their way into the jungle. The American soldiers first sent in a reconnaissance team to check if anybody was still hiding, and to investigate how many were there. They would be able to tell this by checking the toilets and judging from the amount of excrement.

The American soldiers checked the toilets and were shocked. They reported back to their commanding officer.

"Sir, there are over 2000 Japanese soldiers hiding on this island!"

2000 wasn't a number they could be careless with, but it was far too many soldiers to take home as prisoners of war as well. The commanding officer ordered the island to be surrounded and sent his men in for a general offensive attack.

The 400 Japanese soldiers found themselves at the end of an honourable defeat.

ABOUT

The punchline to this joke may not be immediately apparent to those who don't know the *other* urban legend it's playing off; the idea that Japanese people have longer intestines than Westerners.

This idea has been around since at least the 1800s. The theory behind it is that Westerners eat a lot of meat, making their intestines shorter and thicker. Japanese people eat a lot more vegetables and fibre, making their intestines more malleable and much, much longer. Or so the story goes.

In the above tale with the soldiers, the Americans investigate the toilets and intend to judge from the poop levels how many Japanese soldiers are there. Because Japanese people (supposedly) have such long intestines—which the Americans are unaware of—the poop levels are extraordinary and they judge there to be five times as many people hiding on the island than there really is. Cue the Americans being extra cautious and then presumably being very surprised to discover there were only 400 Imperial soldiers and not 2000.

Which begs the question, is it true? Do Japanese people really have longer intestines? Can they confuse a Western army with their astronomical poop levels into believing they have more soldiers than they really do? It's become a kind of general knowledge thing at this point, and you can find numerous anecdotes from doctors who agree that, yes, Asian people tend to have much longer intestines than Western folk. Ask a random Japanese person on the street and chances are that, more often than not, they will also agree. They have longer intestines. It's just a fact, everyone knows it. But is it?

A study by the University of Tokyo was held in 2013 to get to the bottom (ahem) of this myth once and for all. The results of the study surmised:

"In conclusion, we found that there was no

overall difference in the total colorectal length or rectosigmoid length between Japanese and American adults. The total colorectal length increased with age in both the Japanese and American groups."

So, there you have it. Don't let your dreams be dreams. You too can reach the poop levels attained by the soldiers in this urban legend if you just try hard enough. Maybe. At any rate, there doesn't seem to be any scientific basis behind the "common knowledge" hidden in this legend, but hey, the more you know.

Favourite Type

The oldest living man in Japan was asked, "What type of woman do you like?"

The man answered, "It must be older women, of course."

ABOUT

This joke has been passed around for many years now, so long that in most cases the man's name is never mentioned. The oldest man in question here actually refers to Izumi Shigechiyo, who died on February 21, 1986, just shy of turning 121 years old.

He was initially verified as the oldest living person on Earth by Guinness World Records, but that title was withdrawn and given to Christian Mortensen when it came to light that Izumi might not have been as old as he claimed. According to Guinness World Records, the birth certificate Izumi submitted may have belonged to his brother and not him, making him 105 years old and not 120.

Regardless of Izumi's real age, he was a jovial old man and supposedly gave the above answer during an interview shortly before his death. These days it lives on as a popular joke, even if many may not remember who originally said it.

Is That All You Can Do?

A male university student had a habit of twiddling his thumbs. During his job interview he sat with his hands in his lap, rotating his thumbs around each other.

The interviewer, irritated that the man was so fidgety, said to him, “Is that all you can do?”

“No,” the man answered. “I can go the other way as well.” He started rotating his thumbs back in the other direction.

Shortly after the interview, the man was offered a job.

ABOUT

For Japanese university students, *shuukatsu* season, or job hunting season, usually starts around October of their final year, a full six months before they’re expected to start work at the beginning of the business year in April. This is a stressful time, and each year it gets more and more difficult to secure full-time work. To get that elusive job offer you need to not only have the skills required, but you need to stand out from the crowd. Clearly the man’s literal interpretation of his interviewer’s question was enough to make him stand out, because he got the job.

This legend has been around for well over a decade, with the earliest records I can find of it online coming from 2006. It’s no doubt been around for much longer, however, and it’s still a beloved joke shared online today.

Hanage

After being under discussion for several years, an international meeting has finally arrived at an answer to a long-held problem. That problem is "How to express pain in units."

Until now, there has been no accurate way to describe pain, and so a unit of measurement to do so has become a necessity. Finally, an agreement has been reached to accurately describe one's pain levels.

The unit of measurement is to be called "hanage" (nose hair). This measurement name was submitted for proposal by Japan. For this new measurement, pain can be measured as so: One hanage means it is equal in pain to removing one nose hair.

With this, people can easily describe their pain levels in an understandable way.

ABOUT

As the legend states, *hanage* literally means "nose hair" in Japanese. Pain can be a difficult thing to describe, and it varies from person to person. Wouldn't it be neat if there was a uniform measurement we could use to describe our pain?

Rather than on a scale of one to ten, where one person's "3" might be another person's "9," here we have a clear and straight-forward way of conveying how much pain you are in. One hanage is equal to one nose hair being pulled out. Everyone can imagine that, even if they've never done it themselves before. Two hanage is equal to two nose hairs being removed, and on and on it goes. 100 hanage is probably equal to the feeling of somebody's head exploding from the inside, I imagine.

This story is, of course, flagrantly false. Not only do we not measure pain in units of "hanage," but there was no such meeting or proposal to begin with. This story was originally published on the joke website *Yayuyo Kinen Zaidan* on November 22, 1995. It was posted as literal fake news; a joke created by the website. However, in autumn of 1998, information from the fake article was taken and used in a chain letter that swiftly spread throughout the internet. As the letter (or in this case, email) continued to spread, an "official" source was added to give it more authenticity, claiming the information had come from the November 16 morning edition of *The Nikkei* newspaper.

The chain emails slowly gathered new information as they were passed around. One of these changes included the name of the person who supposedly suggested that "hanage" be used as the official measurement of pain worldwide. There were two variations on who this was, however. One said it was a certain professor from the medical department of Hokkaido University. The university confirmed that nobody with such a name worked there. The other claimed it to be a professor from Muroran University… A university that doesn't actually exist.

The legend grew so large that in 2000, it found its way off the internet and celebrities such as Muroi Shigeru (who will show up in later legends in this book) spoke of their suspicions of the story being true. The story was also used for a segment of the variety show *Takarajima no Chizu* in December 2000, where they tried to come up with units of measurement for other things such as "evilness" or "fleetingness."

If you're interested in checking the original article out, it still exists on the *Yayuyo Kinen Zaidan* website. It's been made into a permanent link, perhaps in commemoration of the lofty heights it reached. You can find it at yayuyo.org/?p=9. The page is in Japanese, but it's a small part of living internet history that you can still touch today, well over 20 years after the fact.

CRIME

Lost Girl

A man was driving along a mountain road one night when he saw a young girl run past. Confused, he soon saw a man come running as well.

"Have you seen a young girl around here?" the man asked. Thinking he was the girl's father, the driver pointed in the direction she had gone and continued on his way home.

The next day, the driver heard on the news that there was a murder on the same mountain road he had been driving on the night before. The murderer was the man who asked him about the girl. The girl had, in fact, been trying to escape him.

ABOUT

This urban legend goes by various names, such as "Lost Girl," "The Man Looking for the Girl," or even "Girl on the Night Road." The story is always the same, and possibly one you're familiar with in your own country. A young girl is seen running in a place you would not expect to see (for example, a mountain road at night), and shortly thereafter a man appears asking about her. Innocent and unaware, the witness points the man in the direction and soon forgets about it. The next day he discovers the girl was murdered, and the man was not her father but a crazed criminal. Whoops.

Stories of this legend have been circulating for several decades now. While the above version is one of the most popular told today, there is another version that sees a young woman, not a young girl, running down the mountain. In this case she's covered in blood and the witness (or sometimes witnesses) think that she is a ghost and run from her. Then a man appears and informs them "I just hit a girl with my car. I turned away for just a second and she was gone. Have you seen her?" The end result is the same, but it's thought that this particular version was actually the predecessor to the above.

Around the early 2000s, variations started to claim that the man was actually Miyazaki Tsutomu, the Little Girl Murderer, and the girl he was chasing was his final victim. Others also placed the girl running towards Aokigahara Forest. This version is also quite popular in modern times, but given what we know about Miyazaki's crimes, his victims, and how he was arrested, it's unlikely this urban legend was created because of him, but rather that he was slotted into it after the fact because of the horrific nature of his crimes. Miyazaki's final victim was murdered more than a month before his arrest. He lured her to his car where he then killed her and kept her until her body started to decompose. None of his crimes took place anywhere near Aokigahara, but considering that forest's history, it's not difficult to see why people would add that part to the story as well.

Stalker

A young woman who lived alone was being troubled by a stalker. Someone had been through her garbage, and a man was often seen standing in front of her house, staring at it. However, what bothered the girl most were the silent phone calls. Every day someone called her and then said nothing when she picked up.

One day, at the end of her rope, the woman answered the phone and started screaming. "Leave me alone, you pervert! I'm calling the police!" Silence briefly filled the air, and then she heard a low, deep voice on the other end of the phone. "I'll kill you." Then the phone hung up.

Scared, the woman immediately called the police. The detective who listened to her story told her he would come around and place a trace on her phone. "If anything happens, I'll come right over," he told her and then left.

That night, the woman received another phone call as usual, only this time, it wasn't silent. A man was laughing on the other end. The girl, scared, wanted to hang up immediately, but she did her best to stay on the line so the police could trace it. The man continued to laugh. What felt like forever seemed to pass, and then the girl got a call on her cell phone. It was the detective.

"Listen closely," he said, his voice nervous. "I want you to get out of the house right now."

But the woman couldn't move. What if the man was waiting for her outside? Perhaps suspecting that was what she was thinking, the detective continued.

"We have the results of the phone trace. The phone call is coming from inside your house. The criminal is inside your house!"

Surprised, the woman hung up and ran. She could still hear the man's laughter echoing throughout the house, even with the phone hung up…

ABOUT

Sound familiar? It should. It's thought this urban legend is based on "The Babysitter," a popular American legend which follows the same general plot. It also ends with the strange phone calls coming from the killer who is upstairs on the second floor, calling from inside the house. Babysitters aren't a thing in Japan like they are in America, so the original story didn't have as much appeal to a Japanese audience. By switching the babysitter to a regular young woman, and the criminal to a stalker, the story becomes more familiar for the Japanese to identify with and, once again, a legend is reborn.

If You Had Turned on the Lights

A female university student was drinking at her friend's apartment. When the party was over, the girl started walking home. She soon noticed that she had forgotten her phone at her friend's place. She went back and rang the buzzer.

There was no response.

She turned the doorknob and realised it was unlocked, so she went inside. The lights were off, so she assumed her friend was already asleep. 'How careless,' the girl thought. She considered turning the lights on and waking her friend up, but she was pretty drunk at the party, so instead she fumbled around in the dark for her phone.

"Just came back for my phone," she said and then left once more.

The next day, as the girl was passing by her friend's apartment once more, she noticed a large number of police officers outside. When the girl heard what was going on, she was shocked. Apparently her friend had been murdered. Her apartment was a mess, and the police suspected it was a robbery.

'If only I'd turned the lights on and woke her up to warn her to properly lock the door…' The girl was filled with regret. She mentioned to one of the officers that she was in the apartment the night before. A detective then emerged and told her he had something he wanted her to see.

"We found this message left inside the room. It's been troubling us. Do you by chance happen to know anything about it?"

The girl looked at the note and her face went pale.

"Aren't you glad you didn't turn on the lights?"

The girl's friend was already dead when she returned to get her phone, and the murderer was hiding in the room with her. If she had turned on the lights, then…

ABOUT

Once again, this is a familiar American urban legend that's been slightly modified for a Japanese audience. While stories like this one, the phone call coming from within the house, and even the man under the bed have been around for quite some time, they are relatively recent stories to Japan. While America was developing a tradition of scary tales involving immediate, real-life threats, Japan was more focused on *kaidan*, or ghost stories. Kaidan went through a boom during the Edo Period, and that continued well into the 20th century. Ghosts were the monster of choice for the majority of scary stories, and it wasn't until much later that these American legends started to infiltrate and find a new home.

Some have suggested the reason these "evil men" were able to become popular in modern Japan was because of the growing crime rate and public unrest. In a country traditionally enamoured with the spiritual, these real-life monsters were able to break in and take root thanks to growing public unease. However, most stories needed to be adapted slightly to fit Japanese tastes, and make them more identifiable. With the spread of the internet in the late 1990s and early 2000s, these stories became easy to copy, paste, and share with friends, becoming some of the earliest "copypastas" on the Japanese internet.

Fake Police Officer

One evening after work, a woman was waiting for the elevator at her apartment building. As it descended, she noticed a suspicious man hiding his face as he stepped out.

The next morning, the woman was watching the news when she saw that a murder had taken place in her apartment building the night before. Around lunchtime, a single police officer came to her room trying to find out more information.

"Yesterday evening, did you notice anyone suspicious around here?" he asked.

The woman, remembering the strange man she saw get off the elevator, lied and said, "No, I didn't see anything." She didn't want to deal with all the hassle of admitting she had seen someone.

"Is that so?" the police officer said before leaving. "I'm glad there were no problems then."

A short while later, the woman saw on the news that the suspect had been arrested. When she saw the face on TV her blood ran cold.

It was the police officer who had come to question her.

ABOUT

Also known as "Witness" or "Man on the Elevator," This legend began to spread in 2003 after actress Muroi Shigeru spoke of it on the TV show *Morita Kazuyoshi Hour Waratte Ii Tomo*. It was also published in her book *Anata ga Kowai Suppin Damashi 5* the same year. The story was told to her by her stylist and presented as a true story. Imada Koji, another TV personality, then shared the story with Matsumoto Hitoshi of comedic duo Downtown. Matsumoto in turn then shared the story on his TV show *Downtown no Gaki no Tsukai ya Arahen De!*, as well as his radio show *Matsumoto Hitoshi no Housoushitsu*. He presented the story as a Muroi's actual experience, and many took him at his word. After passing through numerous celebrities and various types of media, a legend was born.

This story was later picked up and recreated by shows like *Yonimo Kimyou na Monogatari* and in the manga *Midnight*. It was also featured in the manga *Tokyo Densetsu*, where a police officer went around warning people of a serial rapist, and it later turned out that the officer *was* the rapist.

Variations of this legend include the man greeting the woman as he gets off the elevator, and in others she even notices blood on his shirt as he leaves. In some versions he comes inside her apartment to talk, in others they talk through the door. In some versions he is arrested the very next day, in others a few days later. Minor details change, but the main points remain the same.

The original story was, of course, a work of fiction told to Muroi by her stylist. However, after being retold several times, as urban legends are wont to do, Muroi herself was disentangled from the story and it became a standard cautionary tale not to trust anyone, even police officers who show up at your door asking for help. After all, they might be criminals as well.

As in other countries, police officers in Japan work in pairs, so if a single police officer shows up at your door then yes, you have every right to be suspicious. But in this case, a story is just a story, and there is no truth behind the legend.

The Terrorist's Gratitude

A woman was walking down the street when she noticed a foreign man holding a map. He appeared to be lost. The woman approached him and asked where he was going. She gave him detailed directions and, in thanks, the man said something to her.

"You are a very kind person. Let me repay your kindness. One week from now, you must not get on the subway. Okay?"

With that, the man left. At first, the woman was confused, but she soon had a sinking feeling in the pit of her stomach and went to the police. The detective she spoke to turned pale and showed her a series of photos.

"Is the man you saw in here?" he asked. Nervously the girl looked through the photos, and then she found the man she helped.

"The people in these photos are terrorists," the detective solemnly informed her.

ABOUT

This version of the legend first began to spread shortly after the September 11, 2001 attacks in New York, when people's fears of terrorist attacks were growing. The reason this particular story mentions a subway attack is likely because of how fresh the Tokyo sarin gas attack was in people's minds. Initially, the man in the story was only referred to as a foreigner, but after the 2003 Iraq War broke out—which Japan was involved in—the foreigner was usually mentioned as an Arab or Islamic man as fears of retaliation grew. The target of the attack varied as well, from an airport to a railway to any number of large, public places, depending on the person telling the story.

This urban legend's roots can be found in a story that was going around in 1999, however; a time when Japan's mind was on potential attacks from somewhere much closer: North Korea. That story goes as follows:

> A young woman was dating a Korean man who lived in Japan. One day, the man suddenly told her, "I can't tell you the details, but I won't be able to see you anymore," and broke up with her.
>
> A short while later, the woman received a letter.
>
> *"On July 25, take your family and go on a trip. Whatever you do, don't be in Tokyo on this date."*

While the date and place changed from version to version, just like the Islamic terrorist, this man warned the woman to get out because he still had feelings for her. In 1999, tensions were high between Japan and North Korea because Japan claimed North Korea had shot a missile over their borders, while North Korea claimed it was a satellite.

Another similar story also exists about the 1995 Tokyo sarin gas attacks. In this one, a young man is informed by an old friend who joined Aum

Shinrikyo not to go to Shinjuku on March 20, 1995. Whether this story was the original, an off-shoot, or simply a similar legend that spread around the same time, no-one knows for sure. What is for certain, however, is that when people begin to fear for their lives, these types of stories will always find a way to come around again.

Tokyo Disneyland Kidnappers

A husband and wife took their four-year-old daughter to Tokyo Disneyland for a day of fun. They took their eyes off her for just a moment, but when they looked back, she was gone. They went to the "Lost Children Centre" and asked them if they had seen their daughter. Unfortunately, she wasn't there.

All the couple could do was wait. However, the staff member's face suddenly turned stern, and he began making calls to various departments around the park. He then ordered all exits and entrances be closed. All except one.

The couple grew even more worried. The staff member took them to the single remaining exit, then turned to them.

"Listen to me carefully. I want you to stay here and watch everyone who's trying to leave the park with a child in tow. They might have already dyed your daughter's hair. They might have changed her clothing. Look very closely, and don't let them slip through."

They slowly came to understand what was happening and carefully checked each person who passed by. Suddenly, they saw a man trying to leave with a sleeping boy in his arms. They almost missed him. The child had short hair, was wearing boy's clothes, and didn't look anything like their daughter. However, looking closer, the child was wearing shoes with a beloved girls' character design on them. There was no doubt about it. Those were their daughter's shoes!

The man was apprehended by the park's security guards. The child had been drugged, but she was otherwise okay and returned safely to her parents. However, it was strange that such a large park would go to such measures to find a single child. There had to be a reason why.

In reality, kidnappings are extremely frequent at Tokyo Disneyland. The large-scale operation is performed by many skilled kidnappers who repeatedly take children from within the park. They take the children to sell their organs on the black market. Of course, the people running Tokyo Disneyland are aware of this, and the police are involved as well. But if the mass media knew, then families would stop visiting the park, and for that reason Tokyo Disneyland does everything in their power to keep the news from getting out.

ABOUT

Tokyo Disneyland, the first Disney park to be built outside of the United States, opened on April 15, 1983, in Chiba Prefecture. The park sees millions of visitors each year and is the third most-visited theme park in the world. Safe to say, it's a busy place, but are people really stealing children to sell their organs on the black market? Is Disney paying the media off so news of this doesn't get out?

This rumour first started to spread around Japan in the spring of 1996. Newspapers were quick on the case, but they were unable to find any evidence of such kidnappings taking place. In fact, it turned out that this legend found its way to Japan via

America as well, as there have long been rumours of kidnappings in several American Disney parks.

There have never been any reports of children actually being kidnapped from Disney, and Disney's in-park security is top notch. On top of their security camera system, they have security officers in the park keeping an eye out for suspicious individuals, as well as the characters and other staff. There are eyes everywhere, and the majority of cases where a child goes missing are settled in less than 15 minutes.

Like many urban legends of this nature, it's unlikely that this legend was designed to bring financial harm to Disney, but rather to serve as a warning to parents that, even in a park as large and popular as Disney, you should keep an eye on your child at all times. All it takes is a single moment and then they'll be gone.

Murder Corps

There's a terrifying fate awaiting those who badmouth the Imperial family. There is an organisation under the jurisdiction of the government called the "Murder Corps," and it is their job to take care of those who speak ill of Japan's Imperial household.

ABOUT

As one commenter so succinctly put it, "If that were true, there would be nearly nobody left on 2chan." That about sums this one up.

On a somewhat related side-note, in Thailand it *is* against the law to insult the monarchy. Article 112 of Thailand's criminal code states that "Whoever, defames, insults or threatens the King, the Queen, the Heir-apparent or the Regent, shall be punished with imprisonment of three to fifteen years." It's not quite murder, but you probably still don't want to do it, and there have been cases of people getting much longer sentences than 15 years for badmouthing the royal family online.

Japan is not Thailand, however, and you're free to badmouth the Imperial family all you want. It's what 2chan spends a lot of its time doing, after all.

Love Hotel Mirror

A young couple went to stay in a love hotel, but they soon ended up getting into an argument over something small. Neither was the type to back down, and before long, the woman threw her handbag at the man's head. He dodged to the side, and the bag crashed into the mirror, smashing it.

The man got even more upset. Now they would have to pay to fix that as well, but the woman remained frozen, staring at it. The man turned around and froze as well.

A video camera was hiding behind the mirror, pointed directly at them.

ABOUT

A love hotel is a short-stay hotel where you can stay for either the night or just a few hours. As the name implies, they're generally used for people discreetly looking to have a little fun in private. At many love hotels, you never come into contact with a single person. You buy your ticket to get in anonymously, you can order food and drinks which are left outside your door, and when time is up, you leave. They are the ultimate in privacy for a country where millions live on top of each other, generations share the same house, and alone time seems like a distant dream.

Love hotels are also a big business. A CNN report in 2009 revealed the industry brought in over $40 billion a year, more than twice that of the anime industry. Considering privacy is one of the biggest draws of love hotels, it sure would be devastating if customers discovered they were secretly being filmed inside their walls…

This legend has been around for a while now, and in 2016, a former love hotel employee addressed it directly. In an interview with RocketNews24, the man claimed that during his entire working history at love hotels he had never once seen a hidden camera… At least, from the management's side.

Hidden cameras are not only a crime, they're bad for business. If anyone so much as mentions in passing that a certain hotel has hidden cameras, customers will avoid it like the plague. The risk of potentially filming customers and selling the footage is far greater than the rewards. Love hotels are already profitable enough as it is, and something like a hidden camera would instantly put a hotel out of business.

Is there the potential that another customer has bought their own camera and installed it inside a room? Of course there's a chance, but again, it's unlikely. They'd need to hide it well enough that no-one would find it, especially the cleaning staff, and they would need to return constantly to pick up the camera and/or footage. Staff clean the same rooms up to six times a day and are very familiar with the surroundings. If anything was out of place, they would notice it. Thus, while it's not impossible, it is highly unlikely.

Another variation on this legend claims that a couple who discovered a hidden camera in a love hotel complained to the owners about it and were quietly paid off to the tune of 3 million yen. Similar legends exist in various service industries, such as burgers that aren't made entirely of meat, and so forth. In this particular case, nobody has ever come out on the record to say they were paid off (and why would they?), but for the same reasons as above, it's unlikely. There's far more money to be made running the business legitimately.

Manhole Thieves

Theft and bag snatching have been on the rise in busy areas like Shibuya and Ikebukuro lately, and it's often attributed to young thieves. However, the number of arrests made for these crimes is relatively low.

The reason for this is because the young thieves are escaping through manholes in the city. In this way they are able to disappear and avoid capture.

ABOUT

Delving into the topic of Tokyo's massive underground tunnel network could take up an entire book of its own (and in Japan there *are* books dedicated solely to the topic), but setting that aside, this legend specifically refers to manholes. This legend wouldn't work for other areas of Japan because most sewers are too small for anyone to escape through; even a large city like Osaka has pipes that are only large enough to crawl or crouch through. Tokyo is the biggest city in the world though, so of course it has massive sewers lying just under the surface that people could escape through if necessary, right?

It's a scene not uncommon in movies and manga. The thieves disappear from sight by dropping into a manhole and make their grand getaway through Tokyo's massive underground pipe system, emerging somewhere far from the scene of the crime in complete safety. But is it true? Can people really escape through Tokyo's manholes?

The answer is "probably not." Manholes don't just lead to big empty pipes that allow people free access underneath the city. They lead to sewers. Full of sewerage. That means they are literally full of water, urine, feces, and all the lovely smells that come with such a combination packed into tunnels and left to stagnate.

Sewer pipes beneath Tokyo vary in length and size. In some areas you can even take a tour if you're brave enough. As you might expect, they smell awful and many leave promising never to go back again. They're full of insects feasting on the filth and to get anywhere you need to make your way through both them and the sludge, leaving you emerging on the other side (if you make it that far) looking and smelling like you literally just crawled through a sewer. Because you did. Not to mention the mere act of getting a manhole open in a city as busy as Shibuya and not have anyone see you is near impossible.

It works well in film, like many other things, but in reality, escaping from police through Tokyo's sewer system is a no-go. You would have an easier time simply disappearing into the massive crowds, and smell better for it at the end as well.

Accident Scammer Fax

A group of scammers is here. Please take note.

1. If you are involved in an accident with any of the number plates below, do not settle at the scene. Call the police right away.

2. Do not give them your name, phone number, address, or company details before the police arrive.

3. Please keep a copy of this in your car.

4. Make sure to inform your family and friends.

< Number plates to be aware of >

Yamaguchi xx-xxxx
Yamaguchi xx-xxxx
Yamaguchi xx-xxxx

If you see a car driving in front of you with any of these number plates, please make sure to drive at a safe distance so if they suddenly brake, you will not hit them. If you discover a car behind you suddenly approaching erratically, take extreme caution. They stop using their parking brake, so you will not see their brake lights!

Our company received this fax. It seems another group of scammers is around. This group causes car accidents on purpose and tries to force settlements on the spot. They operate in pairs. One car in front, one in back. The car in front suddenly brakes, causing the mark to do the same, but with no time to stop, the cars will inevitably hit each other. Then the car from behind will crash as well, meaning the mark has to pay out twice as much damage. This can end up in the tens of thousands. Make sure to be extremely careful when you're driving.

ABOUT

This legend first started making waves in the late 1980s when faxes resembling the above circulated through various neighbourhoods and companies. Depending on the area it was being shared in, number plates varied from Yamaguchi to Osaka to Shinagawa, or other such places that had a strong yakuza image. The majority of places were from western Japan, where the media repeatedly denied that any such groups existed, but in eastern Japan, the rumours were allowed to spread, and many believed them to be true. The list of number plates on the fax grew over the years, and by the end of the 90s had well over 35 cars on it.

As the fax was copied over and over, this slowly produced errors and made the original fax difficult to read. In 1998 and 1999, number plates also began to change from two-digit numbers to three-digit numbers, making the lists even more difficult to believe.

Police began investigating the fax shortly after it was first released, and continued to do so each time new number plates were added. The faxes were especially common amongst taxi drivers, car dealers, and other people specialising in cars; the people who were most likely to be affected by scammers on the road. The number plates on the list largely turned out to be abandoned cars, or cars that didn't exist at all. Police warned people not to be fooled, and that no such group of scammers existed, but the fax continued to circulate, regardless. However, while the number plates on the faxes were mostly dead cars, and there was no such group of scammers, this urban legend *was* inspired by a real-life incident.

ORIGINS

In August 1986, rumours began to spread throughout Hyogo Prefecture that yakuza members were scamming people. Over in neighbouring Kyoto, two months later, a leaflet began circulating featuring the number plates of three known yakuza members. Newspapers at the time connected the two events, and rumours began to spread that the yakuza on the list were involved in scamming people. The police investigated both the cars and members involved, but were unable to find any proof that they had been partaking in scams. By November, a leaflet was being passed around Yamaguchi that featured 19 different number plates, of which several were known yakuza members. The police once more investigated and discovered that the person who created the leaflet was having trouble with certain yakuza members, and so he wanted to extract revenge on them. This didn't stop distribution of the leaflets, however. On the contrary, they continued to spread, with more and more number plates added, the rumour continuing to spread further across the country each time.

The spreading of rumours pre-internet took much longer, but by the 1990s the faxes had been shared around much of Western Japan. Because the majority of the number plates were said to be from Yamaguchi Prefecture, the Yamaguchi Police took over investigations. They concluded that the faxes were the work of a *yukaihan*, a criminal who takes joy in seeing people's reactions to his crimes. The only scamming taking place was that of people who believed the fax to be true.

Still, by 2008, over 20 years after the rumours first began, faxes were still circulating with number plates and warnings to keep an eye out for these scammers on the roads. Some people even believed that the police themselves were circulating the fax so they could warn people of the dangers lurking on the roads, while other suggested it was a government test to see how and where news would spread. The police denied they were spreading anything, of course, but the rumours just wouldn't die.

AT PRESENT

If you can believe it, this fax is *still* being sent around the country, well over 30 years after it first began. The list, seen as recently as February 2019, still includes number plates from Yamaguchi, Osaka, Kobe, and Hyogo Prefectures, all neatly typed out on a computer so they're easy to read. Some even include incomplete numbers or unknown locations to add a little "authenticity" to the lie.

With the proliferation of social media and ease of sharing content, as well as an entirely new generation that potentially haven't yet heard of the original legend, this fake scammer group is a tough one to kill. Of course, the pictures of the fax generally come with a call to action as well, asking people to share so as many eyes get on it as possible. Now that sharing is as simple as the click of a button, it seems almost impossible to stop its spread.

As a sign of the changing times, some have even suggested that people get dashboard cams so they can protect themselves against these scammers. After all, without proof it's your word against theirs. A dashboard cam is certainly not an awful idea, but it's a bit silly for something that a few seconds of research could tell you isn't true.

The scammers don't exist, but their imaginary group proves to be one tough cookie to put down once and for all.

SOURCES

The following is a list of websites visited while gathering information for this book.

3xai Stories: https://3xai.net/
Aru-hen: https://aruhenshu.exblog.jp/
Chicago Tribune: http://chicagotribune.com/
Asyura: http://www.asyura2.com/
Chintai Hakase: http://www.chintai-hakase.com/
Chuugaku Juken no Tame ni: https://ameblo.jp/tekitopapa50/
Dankai Oyaji no Tanpen Shosetsu: https://blog.goo.ne.jp/tudukimituo1028/
Economic Fortune Up: http://xn--zckuap6f2022d35b.com/
Entertainment Topics: https://entertainment-topics.jp/
Excite News: https://www.excite.co.jp/
Explanation of Hisarukigame: http://asunoakiusagi.blog36.fc2.com/
FNN Prime: https://www.fnn.jp/
Folklore wo Kangaeru: http://tkhrsh33.fukuwarai.net/
Fushigi na Chikara: http://fushigi-chikara.jp/
Geino Chojin Densetsu: http://geinousuper.sblo.jp/
Gendai Kidan: http://osi.cool.ne.jp/
Hachimakikou: http://blog.esuteru.com/
Happism: http://happism.cyzowoman.com/
Hatelabo: https://anond.hatelabo.jp/
Healthline: https://www.healthline.com/
ITMedia: https://nlab.itmedia.co.jp/
Japan Culture Lab: https://jpnculture.net/
Jpnumber: https://www.jpnumber.com/
J-Stage: https://www.jstage.jst.go.jp/
Karate Ota: https://www.kenkokarate.com/
Kyota's Wideshow: http://www.kyota.com/
Mimige Bukuro: https://ameblo.jp/sinobu197903/

Minami Akina Official Blog: https://ameblo.jp/akkinablog/
MovieWalker: https://movie.walkerplus.com/
My Game News Flash: http://jin115.com/
Mystery News Station Atlas: https://mnsatlas.com/
Namahahha no Nikki: https://blogs.yahoo.co.jp/namahahha2005/
Naniwa no Futago Boxer: https://ameblo.jp/gachinkofightclub/
Nihon no Toshi Densetsu: http://www.urbanlegend-japan.com/
Nihon Toshi Densetsu: https://xn--9oqx67ab2fnkbmy2he6h.com/
Nikkan Spa!: https://nikkan-spa.jp/
Oricon News: https://www.oricon.co.jp/
Plaza Homes: https://www.realestate-tokyo.com/
Real Hot Space Entertainment News: http://real-hot-space-entertainment.com/
Response: https://response.jp/
RocketNews24: https://rocketnews24.com/
Saga Shinbun: https://www.saga-s.co.jp/
Sankei News: https://www.sankei.com/
Science Daily: https://www.sciencedaily.com/
Senritsu Semaru Hibi: http://blog.livedoor.jp/nanamitohgarashi/
Shinken ni Occult ni Tsuite: http://www.myhomeheating.com/
Shiranai Hou ga Ii: https://anime-toshidensetu1.net/
Society of Automotive Engineers of Japan: https://www.jsae.or.jp/
Statista: https://www.statista.com/
Statistics Japan: http://www.stat.go.jp/
Tabi Chirakashi: http://www.asasikibu.com/
Takajin: https://takaljin.jp/
The Occult Site: http://occult.xxxblog.jp/
The Tsuburu: https://sumaapu0.hateblo.jp/

Today: https://www.today.com/
Tokyo Happy Prank: https://www.youtube.com/TheMaxMurai/
Tokyo Metro: https://www.tokyometro.jp/
Tokyo Urban Legends: http://meru.tv/tul/
Toshi Densetsu Blog: http://yoshizokitan.blog.shinobi.jp/
Toshi Densetsu Hiroba: http://umaibo.net/
Toshi Densetsu Japan: https://xn--japan-9t2hu30gsg3fz4l.com/
Toshi Densetsu Kokontosai: http://sfushigi.com/
Toshi Densetsu Matome: http://totosh.blog.fc2.com/
Toshi Densetsu Matome: http://xn--o9j0bk5542aytpfi5dlij.biz/
Toshi Densetsu no Sekai: http://urban-legend.seesaa.net/
Toshi Densetsu wo Yomikomou: http://d.hatena.ne.jp/folkrorement/
Toyo Keizai: https://toyokeizai.net/
Uwasa no Toshi Densetsu Matome: http://arnomiami.com/
Wikipedia: https://ja.wikipedia.org/
Yahoo! News: https://headlines.yahoo.co.jp/
Yamitsuki Matsumoto: https://yami2ki.com/
Yayuyo Kinen Zaidan: http://yayuyo.org/
Yo ni Habikoru Toshi Densetsu: http://urbanlegend-z.com/
Yonimo Kimyo na Toshi Densetsu: https://yonimokimyo.com/
Youkaiou: https://blog.goo.ne.jp/youkaiou

WANT EVEN MORE JAPANESE HORROR?

Read a sample from *Reikan: The most haunted locations in Japan*, also by Tara A. Devlin.

Kasagi Sightseeing Hotel

Location: Toge-50 Kasagi, Soraku District, Kyoto Prefecture, 619-1303

Before the Kasagi Tunnel was built, before the Lake Forest Resort was built, and before the Love Hotel Century was built, the Kasagi Sightseeing Hotel stood proud alongside the Kizu River in Kyoto Prefecture. Full of people and full of life, customer numbers began to dwindle when other, more easily accessible options opened up.

The hotel was rumoured to be in over 1,000,000 yen debt each month. Unable to deal with this sudden drop in guests and his rising money problems, the owner of the Kasagi Sightseeing Hotel walked down to the first floor, doused himself in oil and lit himself on fire. His attachment to his prized hotel was so strong, however, that even after death, he could not leave it. And he wasn't the only one.

They say the spirit of an old woman haunts the spiral stairs inside the building. If you're not careful, she'll throw you from them too.

On the roof, you'll find the disembodied head of

a young woman, so dreadful that she chases all who see her to their grizzly ends. And every now and then, people lay eyes upon a former employee of the hotel, still in uniform and forever floating the halls of the now-abandoned building, looking for customers to help… or hinder.

These four spirits are the pillars of the haunted Kasagi Sightseeing Hotel. Be careful if you ever try to visit, because it may be your last…

Located close to the borders of Kyoto, Nara, and Osaka Prefectures is the Kasagi Sightseeing Hotel. Situated at the end of a tiny path in the middle of the forest, it closed in 1990 thanks to the emergence of several easily accessible hotels nearby.

One of the most famous stories about the hotel is that the owner set himself on fire near the front entrance and killed himself. Ever since then, people claim to have seen the spirit of a burnt man wandering the building remains, and teenagers entering the building for a spot of midnight fun have reported leaving with burn marks on their own bodies. The building itself has been the subject of arson several times over the years, but there are some who claim that even these attacks were the work of the owner and not bored trespassers.

People report "a sensation like someone coming to greet you" upon entering the old building. One of the supposed "four pillars" of the Kasagi Sightseeing Hotel is a member of staff, although little information is known about this spirit or the person he was in life. People report seeing a man falling from the stairs to the ground, but there's no evidence that this is the same spirit.

The third of the four pillars, however, is said to reside on the staircase. Most of the stairways and floor have fallen apart or been torn down over the years, leaving a large atrium in the middle, and people claim that the spirit of an old woman resides here. Sometimes she's even seen with a little girl, although no-one knows who they are, exactly. It's likely they were once guests of the hotel before it was abandoned, but why they have taken up residence there now is unknown. Visitors to the abandoned building claim that if you look up into the giant gaping hole that was once the stairs, you can occasionally see a white figure looking back down. The area is also famous for floating orbs.

The fourth and most dangerous of the four pillars resides on the roof. Ghost hunters claim that from the fourth floor up, the atmosphere of the building completely changes. The roof now more often than not resembles a lake; water gathers in the rain and stagnates, unable to escape due to the concrete barriers surrounding it. As you may well know by now, Japanese spirits are attracted to water, so it makes sense that the most dangerous ghost of all would be found on the wet rooftop. Rumours abound that her bodiless head will chase anyone who sees her, and considering the state of the building now, that's almost a guaranteed death sentence.

This ghost became especially famous because of her appearance in *Kitano Makoto no Omaera Iku na Hishou Hen*, an occult video featuring the aforementioned comedian Kitano Makato. A young comedian from the Shouchiku Public Entertainment company was walking through the abandoned hotel when a woman's disembodied head was captured floating close behind him.

The building is, of course, off limits, but that doesn't stop people from entering. It has appeared on numerous TV shows over the years, thanks to the infamous ghost head sighting in Kitano Makato's video, and those with a strong ability to see the supernatural claim that the building can look like it is covered in fog at times; this is, in actuality, spirits that have come down from the mountains, attracted by the strong spiritual energy contained within the building.

The abandoned hotel has become so famous thanks to its TV appearances that locals have complained of the troubles that ghost hunters and kids looking for fun have caused. Because of them, the building is deteriorating even quicker, and that's not to mention all the people entering private property by mistake while looking for the hotel. A simple glance at the building reveals walls covered in graffiti, floors rotting and falling apart, and stairs coming apart at the seams. It may not be the Four Pillars of Kasagi Sightseeing Hotel that you really need to fear, but rather the dying building itself.

WANT EVEN MORE?

Also available in *Kowabana: 'True' Japanese scary stories from around the internet*:
Volume One
Volume Two
Volume Three
Origins
Volume Five

Toshiden: Exploring Japanese Urban Legends

Reikan: The most haunted locations in Japan

The Torihada Files:
Kage
Jukai

Read new stories each week at Kowabana.net, or get them delivered straight to your ear-buds with the *Kowabana* podcast!

ABOUT THE AUTHOR

Tara A. Devlin studied Japanese at the University of Queensland before moving to Japan in 2005. She lived in Matsue, the birthplace of Japanese ghost stories, for 10 years, where her love for Japanese horror really grew. And with Izumo, the birthplace of Japanese mythology, just a stone's throw away, she was never too far from the mysterious. You can find her collection of horror and fantasy writings at taraadevlin.com and translations of Japanese horror at kowabana.net.